ISL

Ian Skidmore is a BBC Wales radio presenter and book critic. His published work includes *Escape From the Rising Sun*, *Wildlife in Custody* and *Owain Glyndwr*. He was born in Manchester and now lives in Gwynedd, North Wales.

ISLAND FLING

Ian Skidmore

Star

A STAR BOOK

published by

the Paperback Division of

W. H. ALLEN & Co. Ltd

A Star Book
Published in 1982
by the Paperback Division of
W. H. Allen & Co. Ltd.
A Howard and Wyndham Company
44 Hill Street, London W1X 8LB

First published in Great Britain by
W. H. Allen & Co. Ltd, 1982

Printed in Great Britain by
Anchor Press Ltd
Tiptree, Essex

ISBN 0 352 31023 5

For

LORD and LADY LANGFORD

and their

splendid, hospitable family

'For Auld Lang Syne'

D. P. L. Ganger and Co

Since this book is set in
the future it follows that
there is no comparison with
any incident, place or person
alive or dead. It is, alas,
a work of pure invention.

CHAPTER ONE

When the roar was born it was little more than a sturdy growl, but it grew muscles as it climbed the brandy-washed walls of Sir Huw ap Gryfydd's throat and by the time it had leapt over the stained ivory escarpment of his teeth it was fully grown and armed cap-à-pied.

It would not be correct to describe ap Gryfydd as a throwback. The phrase implies a gentle lob. To propel Sir Huw the distance from the primeval forests from whence he came would have required the propulsion of a guided missile. A tall man, his breadth of shoulder was so immense and his arms so simian he seemed smaller than his actual size. His skin was the colour and texture of moorland scrub and his eyes, which stood out from his face like dish headlamps, were the colour of peat bogs, lit at this moment with Jack o' Lanterns of sheer fury. They simmered wickedly on either side of a nose which mimicked the mountain crags from which his tribe had sprung, club in hand. And the whole terrifying face was marooned in a wild sea of black tangled hair; a volcanic island which could erupt in turn with maniacal glee or, as it did now, the sort of pyrotechnic anger you could warm your hands on. There was about him a distinct odour of smouldering mammoth hair. Anarchic, lewd, devilish and Rabelasian, he was raucously on the side of life and an implacable foe of anyone who disturbed his progress through it. Examine his profile or the ancestral portraits in the gallery of his lair, Plas Becod, for there is little discernible difference in the generations. Indeed, if you took all the two thousand islanders and boiled them down into one six-footer you would get something like Sir Huw ap Gryfydd, which might explain the mystical power which even in the twentieth century he has over them. To make such an examination is to know why the Romans did not invade the two Welsh islands, Ynys Tad and Ynys Becod, over which he holds feudal rights. Becod means pity and is, perhaps, the prime example of the Welsh gift for irony.

ap Gryfydd's present anger had been caused by a letter which now lay on his breakfast table, a crumpled ball in a tundra of congealing porridge. He smoothed it out, and licking traces of porridge from his fingers, read it again:

> 'In the interests of administrative efficiency the Post Office Board for Wales and the Marches agreed at its meeting in Brecon on the following resolutions;
>
> "1. It will no longer be necessary to designate Ynys Becod and Ynys Tad on letters and parcels.
>
> "2. In future, letters and parcels should carry only the name of the addressee, the town or village and the post code. If you do not know your post code I am directed to draw your attention to GPO circular GMYN/YNYS/X/1483721."
>
> 'If you do not receive this letter you should contact me at once at the above address.'

In ap Gryfydd's world it was always the first straw that broke the camel's back and this was indubitably it. ap Gryfydd was intensely patriotic but his patriotism was bounded by the coastlines of his own small islands. While he would have fought to the last gasp in their defence, the rest of Britain, he felt, must make its own arrangements. World War Two had been for him a personal contest to keep Hitler out of Ynys Tad and Ynys Becod. And his views were shared by the islanders.

In consequence the years since local government reorganisation had been uneasy ones for them, and especially for him. Power hungry bureaucrats, reaching out for greater kingdoms to rule, found in him a doughty opponent. He had watched with dismay the gradual erosion of local power on his neighbouring island Anglesey, twenty miles to the north. When the GPO had dropped that island's name he had been furious. Now it was his turn.

Plas Becod, his ancestral home, though impressive, is far from being a stately pleasure dome. Few people outside the owner's close circle of friends have ever been invited to stay there, fewer still have accepted. One who did described the

Plas bitterly as a stone factory for the manufacture of draughts. But whatever its disadvantages as a home it has none as an echo chamber. ap Gryfydd's explosion had left his breakfast table a man-sized roar but its journey down several yards of echoing stone passages nourished it and by the time it reached the butler's pantry it shook the oak door with the strength of a Caliban.

Behind the door ap Gryfydd's manservant, Grout, had been emptying his morning pot of home brew. Now he sighed, drained his tankard, wiped his lips and eased himself out of his rocking chair. Grout had the sort of face of which commemorative jugs are made. There was something ceramic in the lines with which deep indulgence had scored it. Even his complexion seemed more the work of the glazier than of nature. And this startling head rested on a small round body which in turn supported a belly like a spinnaker. But at the roar's command he shot out of the room, two short and chubby legs appearing and disappearing from their owner's view as he hurried down the corridor to play his own vital part in the ceremony that was to follow.

As she opened the oaken door of the Plas the little housemaid, Myfanwy Evans, playing her own role in a frequently observed ritual, thought how much he resembled a runaway Toby Jug.

'Goin' for the cannon ball,' Grout told her. 'I just 'ope that Atkinson don't put too much powder in. We don't want it sinking any more sailing dinghies. 'Specially not today.'

'Yes, Mr Grout, sir,' bobbed Myfanwy. She picked up a rope to which was attached a small sledge with iron runners and handed it to Grout who, pulling it behind him, stepped out of the Plas.

At the moment Grout left the pantry ap Gryfydd stumped out of the breakfast room and up a spiral of stone stairs cut into the tower. Presently, from his position on the foreshore, Grout saw his master appear on the battlements of the Plas where the muzzles of a battery of cannon gaped at the morning.

Some men dance on their hats as a specific against rage, others maltreat the family pet. The more placid write to

The Times. ap Gryfydd preferred firing his cannon. Long practice had brought to the ritual the smoothness of silk. An odd-job man, 'Gunner' Atkinson, whose special care the battery was, came out of his hut on the battlement like an electric hare. He rapidly primed and charged the senior cannon, Meg Fawr, then waited with taper and matches for his master. The ritual never varied. Whenever he was upset at something in the morning post Myfanwy raced to open the main door, ap Gryfydd stomped up the stairs to fire the cannon and Grout stepped out to retrieve the ball where it fell. The Plas at such a moment resembled nothing so much as a complicated mechanical toy. The ritual was not without anxiety for Grout. Gunner Atkinson's hand was often unsteady in the mornings and there had been occasions when the piece had been too generously charged. Properly done the small stone ball landed harmlessly on the foreshore from where it was retrieved by Grout on his sledge. But there had been calamities. Only that summer an inadvertent broadside had sunk a passing sailing dinghy and the summer before a party of five holiday-makers had to be treated for shock at the cottage hospital after a cannon ball had landed squarely on their picnic basket as they sunbathed on a beach on Ynys Tad across the strait.

Happily on this morning the ball which followed the cannon's roar fell harmlessly in a rock pool. It was the work of a moment for Grout to recover it and place it by the front door ready for the boot boy to return it to the battlement.

Half an hour later Atkinson, an admiral now in a shining peaked cap, was in position behind the tiller of the punt which would take Sir Huw, attended by Grout, to the main island and the bi-annual Gathering of the Gorsedd, the island's antique administration, a form of government which it shares with the Isle of Man.

ap Gryfydd did not speak as they chugged across the strait. He was silent as he scrambled ashore on the stone jetty on Ynys Tad and still seething quietly as he climbed into his elderly Land Rover with Grout in the passenger seat. It was not until they had swung out onto the metalled road beyond that he gave tongue.

Changing into top gear as though he was administering a *coup de grace* with a sabre, ap Gryfydd spat rather than uttered the reason for his rage.

'Lord help me to fix them,' he prayed.

It would be, thought Grout sneaking a glance at his master from under his billycock hat, a formidable partnership. For a moment he felt a twinge of sympathy for all the little bureaucrats, wrapped up cosy in all the centrally heated offices in all the newly built county council headquarters in the reorganised world.

'There's a pity,' he whispered to himself, then he pulled down his billycock firmly and closed his eyes as he always did when his master was driving.

When ap Gryfydd, crouched over the wheel, looking like an Old Testament frog, began to hum Grout closed them even tighter. Sir Huw humming meant that he was plotting and plots of the ap Gryfydd boded ill for the plottee. Grout was relieved when the Land Rover coughed to a halt at the Grove of the Gorsedd Stones, where the island's governing body, the Druids, were at this moment assembling.

From the air Ynys Tad and her sister island Ynys Becod resemble nothing so much as a penny farthing bicycle balanced precariously on the rim of mainland Wales. In fact the islands are separated from Britain by a mile-wide channel of fast water and more than a thousand years of passionate mistrust. Aggressively insular they have a prayer which they repeat gleefully and in English, which is rare in that part of Wales, whenever a mainlander comes within earshot of their chapels.

'God bless and God keep the folk of this island
And those other small islands Great Britain and Ireland.'

There is that in their voices which suggests that in the matter of Great Britain and Ireland the Almighty will have his work cut out.

The basic industries of the 1,970 islanders on Tad are farming, tourism and the manipulation of Social Security to finance their activities as fishermen, painters, poets, rustlers and casual workers in the building trade. Compared with

Ynys Tad the black economy of Italy is the palest shade of grey.

On Ynys Becod, separated from the mainland by a vicious tide rip, there are only thirty islanders and the sole industry of twenty-nine of them is to minister to the well being of the thirtieth, Sir Huw. It is an enclosed world and the islanders are loath to give up any of their ancient traditions. So the Gorsedd survives.

Its origins are shrouded in mystery. In form and power it is very like the Tynwald and presumably came to Tad with the same Viking raiders who brought the Tynwald to the Isle of Man. But, like its neighbour Anglesey, Tad was among the last strongholds in Europe of the Druids and on Tad the Viking form of government was grafted onto Druidical traditions.

Like its Celtic forerunner the Gorsedd meets twice a year in a Henge at the exact centre of the island. The first meeting, the Imloc, is held on the 1st of February; the second, at which they were now gathered, Lugnasad, is held on the 1st of August. For the rest of the year the Gorsedd, translating itself into the UDC, meets more prosaically every month at the town hall in the island's capital, Byndrynkin.

The Druids are all chairmen of the various committees and in theory they are re-elected each year. In practice it is seldom necessary to alter the ceremonial white robes which the Druids wear at the Gorsedd. The islanders are a conservative race and only death alters the hierarchy.

Historically the ap Gryfydd of the day is both archdruid and chairman of the UDC and it goes without saying this is both an unchallenged and a life appointment.

The proceedings of the Gorsedd, or the Knowledge of the Oak as they are more correctly described, are in classical Welsh, a more complex form of the language than the patois which is the islanders' daily speech. A very precise ceremonial is followed.

Led by the sword bearers, the archdruid, who carries a sprig of mistletoe, and the Druids form up in the car-park and process to the Grove behind two white bulls, whose presence has led in the past to some pantomime and much slipping and furtive cleaning of shoes. The Druids wear mufti under their robes.

In practice the meeting has an air of a regimental reunion. This is not surprising. The General Staff conducted World War Two in the naïve belief that Sir Huw, then in his early twenties, was O/C 24 Commando. Sir Huw saw the whole thing quite differently. He saw his role, which he practised with great dash and gallantry, as that of a condottiere leading a band of family retainers on chevauchee into France as his ancestors had done for the Black Prince. As, one by one, the elder sons of his father's tenant farmers wangled their way into the army so, one by one, he had them transferred to his command. Both the enemy and the rare general bold enough to visit them were confused by ap Gryfydd's insistence that Welsh should be the sole language of his command. But the persistent success of his unit in any theatre to which it was assigned; the sheer terror its presence inspired in the hearts of the enemy and, if the truth be told, the natives of the occupied country – for ap Gryfydd had little sense of discrimination between foreigners, English, French or German – encouraged the High Command to let ap Gryfydd and his unit get on with the war largely in their own way. Now, forty years onward, he ran the island after very much the same fashion. The elder sons became tenant farmers and in time Druids and councillors, chairing the key committees in the UDC.

In fairness he ran the council with the same mixture of careless benevolence and fierce custodianship he had once employed to run his commando. The ap Gryfydd Groat, a fund administered to assist distressed islanders, is by far the most clamorous call on his personal fortune, to the dismay of his trustees, a much-tried body.

The island's autonomy had been possible because bureaucrats had been bullied into adopting the same policy towards Ynys Tad as the generals adopted to the ap Gryfydd commando. This was due to two factors. The first, enlightened views in the Welsh Office, and the second the diplomatic talents of ap Gryfydd's friend from boyhood, Colonel Alun ap Coch, who was his adjutant in the commando, hereditary

Sword Bearer to the Gorsedd and who was now also his land agent.

Colonel ap Coch, whose family for centuries served as war leaders to the ap Gryfydds, was able if not to control, at least occasionally to curb his friend and employer. He had still been a POW when ap Gryfydd went home in disgust on VJ Day. ap Gryfydd had been looking forward to landing in Japan to avenge the deaths of five cousins in the death camps of the Kwai. For all he knew he had never been demobbed. Certainly he was never promoted beyond half colonel whereas Alun, a dignified and elegant beau sabreur, stayed on and became a full colonel, thus outranking him. This is something for which ap Gryfydd has never been able quite to forgive him.

They met now in the car-park, an incongruous pair, ap Gryfydd a neolithic Elijah in his white robes with the heavy golden torque of his office about his neck, Alun immaculate even in the unbecoming robe of office, his sword point in the ground before him, his long, capable hands resting on the pommel, looking the picture of a Templar knight.

The squire's eyes heliographed wildly when he saw his friend.

'ap Coch, the very fella. I've had the most damnable letter from the GPO.'

ap Coch looked anxious.

'Do let me see a draft of your answer,' he begged. 'Remember that dreadful business with the Special Commissioners of the Inland Revenue.'

It was widely believed among ap Gryfydd's men of business that the letters to the taxman, in which ap Gryfydd complained about his assessment in terms which were frankly libellous, was the direct cause of an increased assessment the following year. But Sir Huw was in no mood for curbs.

'Don't be such a damned old woman,' he barked. 'Perfectly clear to me that someone was on the take. Stood out a mile. Quite right that someone should tell them so.'

'Yes, but did it have to be you . . . ?'

The Colonel sighed wearily because he knew that it did, but Sir Huw hurried on.

'Look, I don't want to talk about it now. Wanted to ask you a question. You've always got your head buried in the darned newspapers. Can't think for the life of me why. Bloody papers! All tits and strikes and pictures of wog uprisings. Gunboat diplomacy, that's what this country needs. My grandfather . . .'

A look of alarm crossed the Colonel's face. The procession had formed and the Druids were beginning to shuffle and paw the ground as they waited for the Archdruid to take his place at their head. The ceremony of Lugnasad was followed by a feast that was in direct descent from the Viking orgy and they were, to a man – there are, of course, no women in the Gorsedd – anxious to take their places at the Board.

'What is it you wanted to know?'

The Colonel prepared himself over a wide range for such inquisitions. There was a library at the Plas but the Colonel was pretty sure that his friend only used it for 'Egyptian P.T.', as he rather rudely described his afternoon nap. He had been educated after a fashion by a series of tutors whom he had bullied unmercifully. None of them had succeeded in any more sophisticated achievement than getting him to read and write, although he had a gift for practical economics that astounded his contemporaries. A question from ap Gryfydd took its pick from a wide field.

'That chap in the seventies in Africa? Rhodesia? Y'know the fella?'

'Zimbabwe,' corrected the Colonel automatically.

'No, wasn't him. Englishman, I believe. Damn fine war record. RAF, as I recall it, but a decent chap all the same . . .'

'No, ap Gryfydd,' interruped the Colonel, 'it's not Rhodesia any more. Zimbabwe, that's its name now.'

ap Gryfydd looked dubious.

'You quite sure? Sounds like a damned curry or one of those frightful dishes they make with bananas. Y'remember that muck the King's African Rifles used to feed us? By the way, what happened to their adjutant?'

By now the stirrings in the Gorsedd procession were becoming audible.

'Ian Smith,' the Colonel said hurriedly.

The conversation was becoming too slippery for ap Gryfydd. The moment he thought he had it by the throat it suddenly twisted in another direction.

'You sure?' he said again, glancing crossly at the Colonel whose memory seemed to him to be fading. 'I thought it was Charlie Owen, went on to command some other regiment.'

'No, ap Gryfydd, Ian Smith was the Prime Minister of Rhodesia. Fell out with us rather badly in, I think, the 'sixties. Declared UDI.'

'That's it,' roared Sir Huw in delight. 'Extraordinary things, conversations,' he went on philosophically. 'Twist and turn like darned elvers. Then just when you're ready to give up, there it is, the very thing you wanted to know – UDI! That's it!' He paused. 'Er, what was it again, exactly?'

'A unilateral declaration of independence,' the Colonel told him. 'Smith and his cabinet believed that Whitehall was governing unwisely so they rather took things into their own hands. Separate kingdoms. That sort of thing.' He smiled. 'Not thinking of starting it on Tad?' he joked. But ap Gryfydd's reply wiped the fond smile from his eyes.

'Why not?' he demanded. 'Sounds a damned sensible notion to me.' He looked impatiently at the Colonel. 'Come along. Can't stand here jawing all day. Gorsedd gettin' restive. Want to get their feet in the trough shouldn't wonder. Feeling a bit peckish meself.'

Before the alarmed Colonel could say another word he had stamped off to the head of the procession. Waving a greeting to his Druids he turned to ap Coch.

'Sword Bearer on Parade!' he roared, and muttering crossly to himself the Colonel, to ironic cheers from the Gorsedd, hurried to take his place at the head of the procession. He was still muttering as the procession moved off but there was no one near enough to hear that the mutterings had become a prayer.

Sword held high before him, shoulders back and treading with military vigour, the words came in rhythm with ap Coch's step: 'Please don't let him be serious . . .'

CHAPTER TWO

When the Gorsedd had formed in its circle, each Druid representing one of the twelve island parishes, Sir Huw took his place on the Gorsedd throne. Colonel ap Coch stood behind him, sword raised, the worried expression still on his face. When everyone was in place Sir Huw shouted the traditional question: 'Shall there be peace?' The answering shout of the Druids, 'Let there be peace!' drowned the Colonel's utterance, 'I profoundly hope so.'

But Sir Huw was lost in the ceremonial.

'I do fence this court in the name of our Sovereign Lady the Queen and I do charge that no person do quarrel, brawl, or make any disturbance.'

An admonitory cough from the Colonel, who could think of only one disturber of the Queen's Peace, broke the silence which followed. Then, one by one, as custom required, the Druids stepped up to relinquish the wands which were their symbols of office, only to step back a few moments later to reclaim them.

As he watched them, twelve men all in their sixties, the Colonel remembered them as he had first seen them. They had been little more than boys then; platoon commanders, section leaders and senior NCOs, their faces blackened, mustering for commando raids. In the eyes of them all he saw the same affectionate loyalty for their chief that he had seen then. In a sudden flash of disquiet he realised that they were still bound together in the brotherhood of their command. Agree to UDI, he thought? If ap Gryfydd asked them they would hi-jack the Cabinet. Even more alarming was the certainty that if they attempted it they would probably succeed. Army service had really been an extension of their tribalism. Their ancestors had followed ap Gryfydds at Crécy and Poitiers. They had arrived at Conwy too late to save Richard II, smuggled to Flint as they were struggling over the wild passes of Snowdonia. But it had been men from Tad who had pillaged the Royal baggage train when Richard's cousin, the Duke of Aumarle, and the Royal Steward, Sir Thomas Percy, had seized it for Henry IV. ap Coch was a medievalist. His greatest pleasure lay in reading the old chronicles. He knew them by heart and he remembered the words of Jean le Creton who had been an eye witness:

'The Welsh who saw their treason here and there opposed them saying "Wretched traitors you shall advance no further this way and shall surrender all the stolen jewels you are carrying away, for the King has not given them to you". Thus were the English robbed by the Welsh. They kept back all the wagons and the harness, gold and silver and jewellery set in gold.'

The Colonel wondered how many of the jewels set in gold had found their way into the coffers of Plas Becod.

Three years later the ancestors of these twelve burly islanders had been out again with Glyndwr when he rose against Henry IV. With him? They had started the whole business. With men from Anglesey, under the leadership of the Twdrs, they had stormed and captured Conwy Castle. That was when the blood feud had started which was still carried on to this day.

Adam of Usk reported the treacherous act by which the Anglesey war lord, Gwillym Twdr, had bought his own freedom and that of his followers.

'Having bound twelve of their number who were very hateful to the Prince, by stealth as they slept after the night watches, they gave them up on condition of saving their own and other lives.'

The twelve had been men from Tad, ancestors of the Druids of today's ceremony. The act was never forgotten and Tad men constantly sought revenge at Anglesey's annual hiring fair.

Even so, when the Twdrs' descendant, Henry Tudor, had made his bid for the throne it was to Plas Becod he had come, secretly, for aid.

Down the long ladder of history the men of Tad had fought on every rung. Remembering the raids of Gryfydd's commando he thought how little they had changed and he groaned. But he was surprised to discover that the groan was accompanied by a quick surge of his own blood. For the ap Cochs, too, had been in every one of those raids and risings.

He dragged himself back to 1985. The ceremony was finishing. In a strong, clear voice, his Welsh at once liquid and commanding, Sir Huw ap Gryfydd, Lord of Tad and Becod, descendant of Welsh kings, Archdruid and chairman of the UDC, was bringing the ceremony of Lugnasad to a close.

Holding high in one hand a huge leather bible as easily as if it were a paperback novel he cried:

'By this book and by the holy contents thereof and by all the wonderful works of God, wrought in heaven above and on the earth beneath in six days and seven nights, you shall without respect of favour or friendship, love or gain, consanguinity or affinity, envy or malice, execute the duties of your office in the protection of these islands of Tad and Becod. So help you God.'

For the first time Colonel ap Coch realised the implications of the oath to which he had sworn every year since his appointment. The last sentence gave Sir Huw a clear mandate. ap Coch hoped that its implications had escaped him. But as he watched his chieftain wave the bible in benediction over his twelve Druids he knew that it had not.

The Feast of Lugnasad is held in the banqueting hall of Plas Becod. Prosaically the Druids, still in their robes, were carried to the jetty by Evans Coach led by Sir Huw in his blue Land Rover, whooping now with joy, waving happily to the islanders they passed on the road. Grout, eyes firmly closed, was once again at his side and in the back sat the Colonel. At the jetty the Gorsedd followed their leader into the Becod launch. Gunner Atkinson at the small brass helm saluted briskly and a group of holiday-makers gaped in amazement at the picture they made.

'Some kind of maritime Eisteddfod,' a solicitor from Liverpool, considered an authority on Welsh culture, observed sagely. 'They'll be singing any moment, Jonquil,' he told his unisex wife, who looked at him in admiration.

In the vast kitchens of Becod Mrs Rose, the head housekeeper, chunky gold bracelets jangling at her wrists, beamed through trendy spectacles – a very with-it woman, Mrs Rose – as she superintended the last details of the feast. In the Great Hall was Grout who had scrambled ashore first and waddled on ahead of the party. He had just completed the inspection of four liveried footmen who stood with trays of drinks in their hands when the doors opened and Sir Huw, robes flying, exploded into the Plas.

Like bloody Merlin, thought Sion Penbran, hired for the day, uncomfortable in his livery and wishing he had time for one more of the Scotches he'd appropriated while waiting in the kitchen. To the wives of some holiday-makers Penbran, a lithe and athletic young fisherman, was one of the island's prime tourist attractions and the end of the season left him tired and tetchy and in need of frequent 'tonics'.

The feast was homely but sustaining. There was Brigant sea trout, Cwm Forest venison and, to finish, huge mountains of the ap Gryfydd Family Pudding, a delicious dish unique to the family in which marrow replaces suet and the whole steaming mountain is topped with hot apricot jam sauce.

There was home-made wine by the pitcher, strong home-brewed beer by the barrel, vintage port with Tad cheese and whisky, champagne and brandy to follow. There were speeches, too, and years afterwards the thirteen guests all vowed that most intoxicating of all that day's offerings was the speech by their host.

During the meal the Hirlwas, the drinking horn of the ap Gryfydd, had democratically accepted every one of the liquids presented to its curved depths. When he stood to speak the hand which grasped it was still firm but Sir Huw listed ever so gently to port. The moorland scrub which was his complexion had burst into bloom, a purple drift that suffused him from whisker to hairline, and the warning beacon of his great nose blazed defiance. Bonfires had been lit in his eyes. His elemental presence swelled before his audience, filling even the huge, sparsely furnished chamber in which they were gathered. His guests watched him in a heady mixture of awe and delight. He was at that stage of inebriation when conversation is easy but pronunciation difficult and his first words lodged timidly in his throat as though reluctant to join the rowdy company. Growling at their recalcitrance ap Gryfydd took another mighty draught from the Hirlwas, and as though desperate to escape drowning in the flooded throat, the words raced out like mariners leaping from a sinking ship.

'Blurry impertinent bureaucrats. Snivellin' penwiping leeches fixed to the back of Wales,' he roared. Even by Sir Huw's standards it was an explosive opening to his ceremonial speech and his audience was riveted. As though surprised by his own vehemence Sir Huw paused, and in the silence his audience could almost hear his thoughts marshalling themselves into some kind of makeshift parade order.

'Got a letter, y'see. Today of all days. You all know how much I look forward to today. Ye'd think today at least they'd keep their damned buff envelopes to themselves. Not a bit of it. Letters on Lugnasad Day, I ask you! Tradition means nothing to the damned sewers.'

Another pause as he invited them with a spread of his arms to share an examination of the enormity of it all.

'And d'you know what they've done now? On this, the island's most sacred day? D'you know? Wiped us off the map. That's what they've done. Listen to this! I ask you!' And delving under his robes he eventually found the crumpled letter which was cowering in the very last pocket he searched. His voice quivering he read the contents to his guests who listened with bays of angry defiance.

'Wales and the Marches, indeed! I'll march the blighters! *Diawl*, I'll run 'em out of Wales with their telephones round their necks! *Arglwydd*, it upset me I can tell you, boys. Tried to clear my mind up on the battery but it was no use. Nibblin' away at me like rats in a bucket. First it was the ten shilling note and the florin. Then the sixpence went. And what've we got now? I'll show you . . .'

Diving once again under his robe and bringing out a fistful of copper coins he hurled them down the table.

'P's. Pockets full of them. Like old ladies on a chara trip!

'Then, damme, they go to work on the names of the counties. Gwynedd, I ask you! Sounds like a blasted bitch spaniel. Dyfed! Clwyd! Hound names, not counties. *Sir Meirionnydd*. That's a name for a county.'

There was yet another dramatic pause as he swept his guests with a glare like the beam from a miner's helmet lamp.

'And now it's our turn. Our beloved Tad swept into the blasted paper baskets under their desks like so much scrap. Humph! Over my dead body . . .'

A noise that sounded like the growl of a wolf pack swelled from his guests. Tankards were thumped on the mahogany with such vehemence that their contents spilled and formed little rebellious rivers round their plates. Sir Huw motioned for silence.

'They don't always get away with it, you know. One or two of you will remember Rhodesia, I've no doubt. What happened there when they tried to change its name, eh?

'I'll tell you what happened. UDI!

'Some chap called Smith, so ap Coch tells me. "Zimbabwe?" he says, and you've got to admit it's even worse than Gwynedd. Sounds like a blasted puddin'. "Zimbabwe?" he says. Decent fella, too, by all accounts. Good war record, I believe. Not that a little thing like that stopped them. Oh, no. "Zimbabwe?" he says. And damn me if he doesn't take the country over. Ask ap Coch. Knows all about it, of course. It was he put me onto it.'

ap Coch looked startled and waved the attribution away anxiously.

'Really, ap Gryfydd!'

'Nonsense,' his friend replied. 'Too damned modest by half. 'Stonishin' well read fella!'

And once again the long suffering tankards were battered in approval.

'UDI for Tad. That's the answer. Owe it all to ap Coch. Never have thought of it myself,' he added generously.

ap Coch's legendary poise seemed about to desert him completely. But ap Gryfydd was a man driven by a vision of the future.

'We'll show 'em,' he promised. 'Defiance, that's what we

want. UDI for Tad. Fortunately the islands are easily defensible. Put a chap on Gallows Point as an OP and if they do try an armed landing I should think we could deal with 'em, couldn't we?'

There was another roar of assent.

''Course we could. And don't forget we ran this island pretty efficiently before government reorganisation. If some damned RAF type can do it, I'm sure we can.'

'But ap Gryfydd,' objected Colonel ap Coch, 'Smith lost. He was kicked out of office. It *is* Zimbabwe.'

'Don't be so confounded defeatist. Poor devil only had native levies. We've got 24 Commando. Besides, what do the RAF know about ground fightin'? Excellent chaps, of course. No denying it. But, my dear fella, they're not trained for it. We are.'

'But we're also, all of us, over sixty.'

'So was Churchill,' rejoined ap Gryfydd.

And with a final triumphant sweep of the table with his great blazing eyes he slumped down in his chair and drained the Hirlwas.

From the far end of the table Colonel ap Coch looked round his fellow guests with resignation. The idea was spreading like Foot and Mouth. He noticed that in the bubble of excited conversation not one voice was raised in dissent. Nothing could have been more unilateral than Ynys Tad's declaration of independence. Wearily he signalled for Sion Penbran to fill his glass.

'*Diawl,*' said Sion, as he poured a brimming tankard of Cwrw Becod. 'Done it now, he has!

'Won't affect my Social Security, will it, Colonel?' he asked anxiously.

CHAPTER THREE

Like the Medes and the Persians the Gorsedd made its decisions twice. Once when drunk and again when sober.

Accordingly, some days after the euphoria of the Lugnasad Feast, the Gorsedd reassembled in the business room of Plas Becod.

ap Gryfydd was puzzled. He knew that on the night of the Feast ap Coch had opposed the idea as wild, dangerous and impractical and he expected recriminations and argument. But none had come. When he arrived for the meeting his friend had seemed subdued, his greeting quiet. He surprised ap Gryfydd by telling him:

'I've prepared a Sit/Rep. Thought you might want it.'

'Obliged,' replied ap Gryfydd, and called the meeting to order. The gathering took on the atmosphere of a wartime briefing. ap Gryfydd had been exercising his hounds and was still dressed in rat-catcher and carrying a massive Victorian riding crop. He used it now to rap on the table round which ap Coch and the twelve Druids were gathered. When he spoke his voice, crisp and business-like, took his hearers back more than forty years.

'Thank you, gentlemen,' he said. 'At Ease.'

ap Coch admired, not for the first time, his chief's sense of theatre.

'I propose to conduct this meeting in a form we are all accustomed to. So without anything further from me I'm going to call on Colonel ap Coch to give us an Appreciation.'

With an agreeable sense of *déja vu* ap Coch shuffled his papers and put on his spectacles.

'Objective. To secure the islands of Tad and Becod to a state of unilateral independence,' he began, glancing only briefly at his papers. 'Factors affecting. It is important, firstly, to achieve control of the approaches to the island. There are three. Firstly, by air. In practice that means the landing strip of the Tad Flying Club. Secondly the jetties of

Byndrynkin, Ynys Becod, Pendyn and Beauville, and the port of Caerholi with its Irish ferry terminal. Thirdly the holiday beaches of Llandwynadl, Aberbrigant and Goch Strada. As you know, the rest of the coastline is mainly cliff. These could be patrolled by sea and two-man land patrols.

'Resistance. The oil terminal at Wrystwych. This represents a major investment by international oil companies and it is likely that opposition will be encountered from the security guards. Also the nuclear power station. My understanding is that the night time manning of this installation comprises only four men. I understand that two have family connections in this room so that containment should present little difficulty.

'Civilian Police. Chief Superintendent Jones was, of course, RSM of our commando and it is within my personal knowledge that he was unhappy with the decision to amalgamate his force of eleven men with the larger North Wales Constabulary. Perhaps you could have a word, ap Gryfydd?'

ap Gryfydd nodded. The Tad Shilling, as the force of twelve 'coppers' was called on the island, was very touchy and proud of its individuality. He made a note on his pad.

'Likely Reaction of Civilian Population.' ap Coch paused as he remembered Sion Penbran on the night of the feast. 'We fourteen here today represent the largest group of employers on the island and we can, no doubt, answer for our work forces. The self-employed on the island are largely in service industries. I can see little change in their lives. Frankly, the problem is Social Security.'

ap Gryfydd waved a hand.

'No worry there,' he assured them. 'Met a chap once from *The Times*. Told me the only official building left functioning in the Falls Road was the Social Security office. And whatever was going on the government made sure that was fully funded. Even though, according to the chap from *The Times*, the IRA used it as a pay office.'

The Colonel stacked his papers.

'That's about all, then. Preliminary Assessment, of course. Judging it purely as a military operation for the transfer of power it's eminently feasible. But I feel I must point out that we will be operating against the law of the land. And the penalty for what we plan to do could attract a sentence of death. Traitorous behaviour, as such a thing might be seen to be, remains a capital crime.'

The Colonel peered over his half-rimmed spectacles.

'Any questions?'

Twdr Plas Drynkin, a former platoon commander, was one of the biggest tenant farmers on Tad. It was said that he still had the first pound note he had ever earned. Knowing smiles were exchanged when he asked:

'What about the banks?'

'No problem,' ap Gryfydd told him. 'Money will still circulate on the island and we'll make sure that the bank – there is, as you know, only one – doesn't take any off. For practical reasons of policy the Wales and West Midland Bank will have to continue to fund their branch here so that cheques can be honoured. And, of course, there's the Social Security cash.'

The commando's demolition expert, Evans Dynamite, sheep farmer, special constable and Crowned Bard of the island Eisteddfod, had been testing in his mind the opening lines of a Tad anthem. Reluctantly he abandoned the complexities of the verse to bring his attention to more practical matters.

'Must we secure the oil terminal? It would make a lovely bang.'

'Out of the question,' ap Coch told him hurriedly. 'Besides, my reading is that so long as we preserve the status quo we'll have no problem with the oil company after we've secured the installation. The explosion at Bantry Bay and the oil slicks of the 'seventies have, as you know, made a lot of local authorities reluctant to allow the building of such installations. Milford Haven, Anglesey, and Tad are the only authorities in Wales who have offered them a home. And don't forget they spent millions laying our pipelines to link with the Anglesey pipe. I can't see them abandoning such a costly investment.'

'There's a pity,' said Evans Dynamite. 'Make a lovely blow, by damn.'

'*Chwarae teg*,' remonstrated Twdr, who was also chairman of the Tad UDC finance committee. 'We could charge them a landing tax.'

In 1980 the oil company payments agreed with the council had been grabbed by central government under the provisions of the Local Government Bill. Until that became law the island had been getting £200,000 a year. Five years later the oil company was paying a £2,000,000 levy for its Tad terminal but it was all going to central government. Both Anglesey and Tad had opposed the bill bitterly but without success. To Twdr it amounted to an act of personal theft for he exercised a parent's eye over any money he administered and it rankled.

ap Gryfydd beamed approval.

'Good thinking, Plas Drynkin. And a tourist tax too. So much a head for adult visitors. Been advocating it for years.'

'Think the visitors'll pay it?' asked Twdr, enchanted as always at new sources of revenue.

'They will when they realise there's no tax on the island. Whisky at 7/6*d* a bottle. Fags at 2/– for twenty. Wouldn't you pay an admission charge for the run of a duty-free ship?'

'No duty?' The question leapt from every throat.

'No income tax either?' asked Twdr.

ap Gryfydd smiled, a slow, sly smile.

'No VAT neither. Didn't pay it in Rhodesia, did they? And what about the Isle of Man and the Channel Islands? We'll have to fix a local tax like they do, of course, but we'll keep it low.'

Siethenyn Pritchard, Accountant, had not joined in the discussion until this point. He had been taking deep draughts of the Cwrw Becod which had been thoughtfully provided. A mountain of a man, shaped like the barrels he venerated; if there had been a Brewer's Consumer Panel for Wales Siethenyn would have been its chairman. His brother, Glyn, who farmed the family acres, sat next to him. A thin, puritanical teetotaler, he tolerated his brother's lapses in deference to his wizardry with the farm accounts, but he did not approve of them. He groaned as Siethenyn leaned forward.

'Licensing laws?' he queried, hardly daring to hope.

'Same thing applies,' ap Gryfydd assured him. 'They were part of the Defence of the Realm Act but we'll no longer be part of the realm. So we'll keep continental hours, of course.'

A rapt expression crossed Siethenyn's face, which drew an impatient snort from his brother.

'Continental hours! *Duw!*' he sighed seraphically. 'Think of that!'

'Popular with the islanders, you think?' ap Gryfydd asked.

'Oh, yes. Yes, indeed, Sir Huw,' Siethenyn told him. 'Good as three Sundays to the week.' He stopped as another thought struck him. 'Open on Sundays, too?' he asked.

His brother snorted again and then again when ap Gryfydd, who was plainly in a giving mood, said: 'Why not?'

'Why not, indeed?' said Siethenyn, journeying far beyond his wildest dreams. 'Think of that, now. Sunday opening. Not independence. Bloody paradise, you ask me.'

ap Coch broke in on his reverie:

'What about the islanders, though? Any thoughts anyone?'

Meredith Bread Rolls spoke now. He owned the island's only corn mill and a small but profitable chain of cottage bakeries. His unusual nickname came from the venerable Rolls-Royce in which he delivered bread. His two sons were known respectively as Tommy Bun and Willie Bun. Meredith had bought the Rolls at a mainland auction, shipped it over in pieces on the small ferry steamer, reassembled it and had since driven it proudly round the island's twenty miles of rutted roads. It was, of course, a prisoner of the island but it was a giant of a status symbol. And through the customers it brought Meredith heard all the island gossip. The others who knew this listened attentively when he gave his opinion.

'Doubt if they'd notice the difference. Half of them have never been further than Caernarfon. Don't want to either. They'll be happy so long as the visitors keep coming. Rely on visitors. All cash, see. No tax. Still, if there's no tax anyway that wouldn't be a problem either.'

At the far end of the table sat a small silent man. Like

ap Gryfydd, Eddi Pant Ddu was a survivor from an earlier, wilder time. Smaller than all his fellow Druids he was yet the strongest. He wore two waistcoats even in August under the khaki dust coat that was his only concession to summer. In winter he exchanged it for his army greatcoat. He looked like an inexpertly carved stone idol that had weathered badly. An oily cloth cap grew on his stone head like a strange tweed fungus. Few had seen him without it. He had been the unit transport sergeant in the commando and the cap had served with him throughout the war to the chagrin of Regimental Sergeant Major Jones. Before he spoke he made a curious whinnying noise in his throat as though he were being cranked. The others waited expectantly.

'Common Market?' he presently asked. 'In or out?'

'Out,' said ap Gryfydd firmly to a roar of approval from the entire table. All the island farmers ran sheep and the French boycott had hit them badly.

'No more Frog apples,' said ap Gryfydd. 'Worth it for that alone.'

'Perhaps we could buy their butter cheap?' ventured Meredith Bread Rolls. 'Just like the Russians.'

'Good about the Common Market,' said Pant Ddu, who had entered the European Community grudgingly, believing that he would have to drive his cattle to Brussels. Since Pant Ddu was among the many islanders who had never even been to Caernarfon this erroneous belief had plagued him for months.

'If I may speak?' Colonel ap Coch, who had been ticking off items on his agenda. 'Since you are all clearly set on this mad enterprise I think we should discuss the possible reaction of the council. I believe we must go through channels. It's hopelessly illegal, of course, whatever we do. But we'll have greater sympathy outside, I believe, if we at least make some concessions to proper form and procedure. What I mean is it will look better if we appear to be acting with the approval of full council. Any chance of getting it? John Parry Millionaire, you're leader of the council, how do you read it?'

John Parry Millionaire got his nickname from the caravan

site which he had opened on barren cliff-top land at the edge of his farm. Asked about it he invariably answered: 'Best crop on the farm is caravans. Only way a farmer can get to be a millionaire, barring Foot and Mouth, of course.'

He was an equally shrewd observer of the factions which made up the council.

'Well, Colonel,' he said, considering. 'Plaid Cymru'll be furious, fair play, they didn't think of it themselves. Beats fasting any old day. They'll claim it was their idea, of course. They always do. But they'll have to approve. Nearest they're likely to get to Home Rule. Labour will be against it if Plaid's for it. And if Labour oppose it naturally the Conservatives will support. So will the Independents and Will Looms Lloyd George here can speak for the Liberals. Him being the only one.'

Will was a wiry man whose head seemed somehow too large for the slender neck which carried it; a neck so thin and elongated that the brick-coloured head looked like a Mardi Gras balloon. He ran the Groeslon Inn, the oldest hotel in the island's capital, Byndrynkin. A natural perversity and a love of argument, which had twice led his wife to bar him from his own pub, had determined his choice of party. As Siethenyn Accountant said, 'If another Liberal came on the council he'd leave.'

'The Liberals are with you to a man,' he assured ap Gryfydd.

'Then I suggest our next move is to lobby for support and when we're sure of a majority one of you can propose a resolution calling for UDI,' ap Coch said. 'Not the chairman, I think; though he might speak in favour. Say we aim for the next meeting which is the first Monday in September. That gives us three weeks by my reckoning.'

'Right,' said ap Gryfydd. 'All agreed?'

All were.

'Any more questions?'

There were none.

'Then I declare the meeting closed.'

He got up and as the others filed out of the room he beckoned Colonel ap Coch.

'Alun, can you stand fast a moment? Like a word.'

'Of course,' said the Colonel and resumed his seat.

When they were alone ap Gryfydd brought out an enormous decanter of the island whisky, distilled, ap Coch knew, in great secrecy on a farm in the interior. He poured two hefty drams and pushed one towards his friend who took it and sipped it cautiously.

ap Gryfydd came to the point at once.

'Never expected to carry you with me. Got the feeling at the Gorsedd you were against the whole enterprise.'

'I am,' said ap Coch bluntly. 'I think the scheme is total madness.'

He caught ap Gryfydd's inquiring look.

'Circumstances alter cases, though.'

'Circumstances?'

'I hadn't meant to tell you this but I suppose someone must know,' the Colonel went on, choosing each word with care and producing it slowly as though reluctant to part with it. 'Y'know I went to the damned specialist again?'

ap Gryfydd nodded, immediately concerned.

'Well, I had his report yesterday. Don't want to beat about the bush. Fact is I may not be around all that much longer. About five years at the outside. No need for sympathy. Been hellish lonely since Rosemary died. Still, it was a bit of a shock. I suppose when we all got out of the war in one piece I'd rather thought of myself as immortal. Seen it happen to others, of course. But it was always the other chap, if you see what I mean. Well, my lad, I thought. Your turn now. And then I started thinking how much fun it had all been. And, d'you know, I found that the part I'd enjoyed most was the war. Hellish frightening, of course, but fun too in a curious way. Damme if that wasn't what I reckoned I'd miss most. Found myself wishing for just one more war before I drew the last card. Rum, really. And, well, it suddenly struck me. We've got one here. Not the Ardennes, of course. More like that thing that Jorrocks said about hunting. What was it? "All the excitement of war with none of the attendant dangers." Something like that, anyway. So I thought to hell with it. One last bit of fun before I go.

'And it will be, won't it, Huw? Fun, I mean?'

There was a tone in his voice that in anyone but him might have been mistaken for pleading. And when his friend poured them each a second hefty dram ap Gryfydd's eyes were swimming. But he raised his glass to ap Coch and in a voice unusually gentle he promised:

'Oh, it'll be that all right. My word on it. *Hwyl fawr!*'

'*Hwyl fawr!*' replied ap Coch, smiling slightly, and the subject was never mentioned again.

CHAPTER FOUR

'But they can't . . . can they?' the Prime Minister wailed when the news arrived, looking wildly for reassurance at the little worried knots of senior civil servants who had been called to the Cabinet Room of Number 10.

'I mean, it's unconstitutional, surely? And it makes us look such fools,' the PM added bitterly. 'The French will have hysterics.'

The news that Ynys Tad had issued its declaration of independence could not have come at a worse time. A trade delegation from Zimbabwe was in Britain and on the point of signing a large arms contract.

'They'll think we've done it on purpose,' the Prime Minister prophesied gloomily. 'It's not a stunt by the opposition, is it?'

There was a general shaking of heads and the Prime Minister's face, which had lit up at the thought, darkened at once.

'And in election year, too. We really cannot afford the bad publicity.'

It was not a stunt. Ynys Tad UDC had voted overwhelmingly in favour of UDI with only four abstentions. These were from Elders who sat in the Big Seats in chapels on the island. They approved of independence, indeed they might not have drawn the line at bloody insurrection. But they were violently opposed to continental licensing laws and the thought of the public houses on Tad opening on Sundays was abhorrent to them. ap Gryfydd accepted their resignations from the council with genuine regret. Otherwise the lobbying had been brilliantly effective. In the weeks before the meeting Tad had been transformed into an outdoor Tammany Hall. ap Gryfydd, ap Coch and the twelve Druids visited every councillor making deals and promises and calling in past favours. Some they visited had been apprehensive, others frankly sceptical, but one by one they were won over. For the farmers among them it was the prospect of getting out of the Common Market which was the most compelling argument. For shopkeepers the spur had been the ending of VAT; for the self-employed reducing income tax carried a high priority. Those whose votes were won by the thought of the new licensing laws and the reductions in the price of tobacco and spirits took care that their wives did not know what had influenced them. They talked sagely of the benefits of independence but they thought of 'spree'. The word came from an old Welsh root – *asbri* – which described the habit in earlier days on the island when upright pillars of the community were granted occasional indulgences to go on 'sprees' of drunken behaviour and quiet riot.

But above all things it was the speech that Sir Huw ap Gryfydd made which put the council firmly behind the UDI resolution.

'Quite improper,' tutted the Prime Minister. 'He should never have spoken in favour of the resolution. Chairmen are required to be impartial.'

The PM had served long and diligently in local government, rising from failure to failure before getting into parliament and eventually becoming the Queen's First Minister. Drawing on this vast experience Britain was now governed as though she were a Metropolitan Council. But not even Sir Huw's worst enemies could accuse him of impartiality. There were no greys in the palette of his personality, only primary colours. A cunning orator he altered both style and wardrobe to suit his audience. In his white robes of the Gorsedd he had been the tribal chieftain, all fire and Celtic magic. At the meeting which followed at Plas Becod the rat-catcher with riding breeches and boots and the brusque soldierly manner had conjured up the staff officer. For the council he stepped into the role and costume of an elder statesman. The huge knot of his silk tie was imprisoned by a pearl pin beneath the wings of a butterfly collar. In his black coat and striped trousers, a gold Albert across his waistcoat, he would have won the most reactionary heart. When he rose to speak his voice was unusually soft and under firm control. He had learned a great deal from listening as a young man to the election speeches of Lloyd George and later, with grudging admiration, to Aneurin Bevan.

The Prime Minister looked down with a fine mixture of distaste and envy at the spread of newspapers on the polished mahogany of the Cabinet table. Most carried banner headlines which ranged in wit and inventiveness from the *Daily Express–Mail*'s 'Island Fling', through the *Sun*'s 'U.D. Aye. Aye!', to the *Daily Mirror*'s 'Island of Viet-taff', a play on words unused since the Investiture of Prince Charles fifteen years earlier. Even the *Star* carried three paragraphs of the story, headlined 'Booze Island Bonanza', under the Page One Nude, who was wearing for the occasion a tall Welsh hat. By the mid-'eighties only the *Guardian* hid its obligatory nude on Page Three.

The more serious newspapers reported the speech verbatim, an honour not even the *Daily Telegraph* awards lightly.

The Prime Minister picked up the *Express–Mail*, and skipping the first four paragraphs of general introduction, began reading the speech intently.

'Sir Huw,' the PM read, 'an ex-Commando leader, told the council that since local government reorganisation in the early 'seventies the island's control over its own way of life had been gradually eroded. He pointed out that islanders had never been worse off than they were now.

'He told the council: "There has been an alarming drop in standards and I believe there is a widespread view that this little island should be given back all the powers that were lost under reorganisation". (Cheers.)

'"Members will recall,"' the Prime Minister continued reading out Sir Huw's speech, '"that in 1980 I passed on this view, at their recommendation, in a memorandum the Clerk prepared for Mr Nicholas Edwards, the then Secretary of State for Wales. That was the time, you will recall, when central government was framing the Local Government Planning and Council Bill. Dammit, all we asked for, like Anglesey, was a restoration of county status. We should have known better. Those Shylocks in Westminster hoard power like misers."'

Here the Prime Minister broke off and sniffed audibly.

'What does the damned fella think we take all that trouble to get here for?' that sensitive personage demanded. 'All those hecklers and constituents.'

'"And gold, too,"' the report continued. '"They like that. Don't forget the oil company levy. They grabbed that, too. Two million pounds we could have used to make this island a better place to live in.

'"And what a patronising letter we got back," Sir Huw continued. "D'ye remember it? Never mind, I've got it here."

'Sir Huw then produced the letter and read it to the council. "Listen to this: *I can well understand the feeling of loyalty the people of Tad have for the pre-1974 structure of local government but I am afraid that I can hold out no prospect of county status being restored to the island.*"'

The Prime Minister looked balefully over the top of the paper. 'Why can't I get my speeches as fully reported as this? Get me Saatchi's. And I want to see the Secretary of State for Wales and the Defence Secretary. The damned fella will be wanting a party political broadcast next, I shouldn't wonder.'

The report went on, still quoting Sir Huw.

'"Understand, can he? I don't think he can understand. But he will. By my whiskers, he will. Because there's a way we can make him understand. Smith's way. UDI!" (Louder cheers.)

'"Whose island is it, anyway? Who fought the Vikings for it and the *Sais*? And who was that damned Henry VIII with his Act of Union? The progeny of Anglesey *brân* (crows). Typical Twdr trick. Conwy Castle all over again." (Prolonged cheering and shouts of "Go Home *Sais*".)

'"Welsh Office reaction was predictable, of course. They've been walking over us for centuries. Would it have hurt, though, to make Tad and Anglesey a special case? No, by damn, it wouldn't.

'"Fellow councillors, I believe we have been fobbed off once too often. And this directive from the GPO is the last straw. Wipe out the name of our lovely island, would they?" (Shouts of "No, by God!" and more cheers.)

'"By God is right," went on Sir Huw. "We've been on our knees long enough. Knees are for praying to the Big Man. Not being preyed on by Whitehall. Get up off our knees, I say. Get on our own two feet, planted firmly on our own dear soil. And shout so the whole world can hear. HOME RULE FOR TAD AND TO HELL WITH THE COMMON MARKET!"

'At this point,' the story concluded, 'the entire council rose to its feet cheering and throwing agenda papers into the air. The meeting ended with the singing of Land of My Fathers.'

The Prime Minister let the paper fall.

'What can I do? Televised cabinet meetings, with co-opted members from the TUC; two World Cup wins in a decade; twenty-four hour TV; a fifth TV channel for Cornwall and the Isle of Man; free transport for Flying Pickets; hot soup for student demonstrators and prisoners' pensions. What more do they want?'

The voice was piteous now.

'They can't do it, can they?'

'I'm rather afraid they have,' a senior civil servant answered. 'The question is, Prime Minister, what are you going to do?'

'Me?' asked the Prime Minister, showing consummate statesmanship. 'I've already done it. I've sent for the Secretary of State for Wales. His pigeon, you know.

'And heads may roll,' the PM added, looking enigmatically at the suddenly discomfited faces around the room.

Meanwhile on Tad the occupation was proceeding swimmingly, literally in the case of the Oil Terminal which was captured with only a skirmish by island trawlermen. They swam ashore and overpowered the security police from the rear. Wisely Colonel ap Coch had also enlisted the services of Meurig Raisin Balls, the doyen of the island poachers, who had the trick of putting both pheasants and game-keepers' dogs to sleep with doses of valium slipped inside raisins. The oil terminal guard dogs slept for twenty-four hours.

The first position to fall into the hands of the island forces had been the Tad Flying Club. Opposition crumbled when a small hand-picked force, led by Colonel ap Coch, approached the proprietor, Wing Commander Geoff Welch,

DFC, and suggested adjourning to the nearby Bull's Head for a pint of something brown and foaming.

Welch had come to Tad after a very active war flying Spitfires. With his gratuity and a legacy he bought two Tiger Moths and a Rapide and took a lease on an abandoned fighter bomber station which the RAF had built on Tad during the war. Between taking holiday-makers on round island flights, running a charter service to the mainland and teaching the more adventurous islanders to fly, he was making a handsome competence. A deeply committed bachelor, he lived in splendid isolation in the Officers' Mess on the airfield with a parrot called Goering, which he kept for conversation, and a Welsh terrier, Taff, probably the best fighter at its weight that Wales has produced since Tommy Farr.

It was in appreciation of these fighting qualities and the notoriously short temper of Goering that the invasion force had suggested adjourning to the snug, raftered bar parlour of the Bull's Head.

'Though, come to think of it,' said Meredith Bread Rolls, 'I don't know which is worse. Getting your finger bitten off by bloody Goering or your head bitten off by Barney.'

Barney the Bull, the legendary landlord of the Bull's Head, ran a tight ship.

Welch was a handsome man. Although his hair was silver, his face was boyish, lit by sparkling blue eyes. With his loosely knitted silk scarf and his leather flying jacket, he took ap Coch, who liked him enormously, instantly back to the 'forties.

Invaders and invaded established a bridgehead in the regulars' corner next to the serving hatch and prepared to defend it against all comers.

'What can I do you for?' asked Welch.

'Actually,' said ap Coch, 'we were rather hoping to occupy your airfield.'

He paused courteously to allow Welch to choke on his ale, then, when his complexion resumed its normaly healthy tan, he explained about UDI. Welch listened with growing delight.

'What an absolutely marvellous idea,' he said at last.

'You don't mind, then?'

'Mind? Mind? I've been longing for something like this for years. In fact, my dear old Colonel, you've just recruited yourself an air force.

'My members will be absolutely delighted. They're getting a bit cheesed off with bumps and grinds and stooging around over the island. I'll start combat training on Saturday.'

'We don't want anyone hurt,' said Siethenyn Accountant. 'I mean not real bullets and shooting them down or anything.'

'No, I do see that,' replied Welch. 'I was thinking more of patrols. Qui Vive and all that. I'll work out a roster for daytime cover.'

Colonel ap Coch was enjoying himself hugely.

'What sort of air power can you give us?'

'Well, there's the Moths. Grand old buses! And the Rapide, of course, for supplying drops. The Club has three Piper Comanches, all air-worthy. Have to get the committee's OK but I don't anticipate much trouble there. And there's Mrs Batty's Piper Cub. I think we can count on that. Total of seven aircraft. Two-hour patrols, twelve-hour stand-downs for maintenance and recreation. Should see us through.'

'We're more concerned about the other side using your runway to land troops,' ap Coch told him, 'though the patrols will be invaluable.'

'Too short for the sort of aircraft they'll use. If they bring helicopters we can roll oil drums onto the strip. I'll need ground bods for that, of course, on permanent standby.'

'The boy scouts are going mad to help. Sir Huw's Commissioner for the island,' Will Looms pointed out.

'Just the chaps, they can camp in Acre Meadow,' Welch told him.

Even so long after the event the parallel negotiations which led to the occupation of the Nuclear Power Generating Station still carry a security embargo. They were of a delicate family nature and involved, it has been said, certain promises about not disputing the will of a shared aunt, recently deceased. There was also, it has been hinted, an exchange of guarantees over the disposal of a Welsh dresser, the ownership of which had been the cause of dissension between Twdr Plas Drynkin, who led the Tad forces, and Williams Hiroshima, the foreman of the Power Station which supplied electricity to the North Wales grid.

Suffice it to say that on the eve of Tad Day One a gate in the Power Station fence was left open and the staff of four engineers, out of concern, presumably, for government property, agreed to work under the island's new government. When next morning Mr Tibbs, the manager, arrived the takeover was complete.

By nightfall on Tad Day One Colonel ap Coch was able to report to Command HQ that all the objectives had been accomplished: patrols had been set up and supremacy in the air achieved.

'And what about you, Alun? How do you feel about it now?' asked Sir Huw.

'Bloody marvellous!' replied ap Coch.

CHAPTER FIVE

Each in his own little bed, Meredith ap Owen and Gareth Jenkyn dreamed of revolution. They dreamed of it every night of their lives. It was almost the only time they ever agreed, though their dreams differed in content. Meredith, headmaster of Ysgol Ifor, dreamed of driving the Saxon hordes back over the border, of televised Eisteddfods and the Herald Cymreig in every letter-box. He spoke Welsh on the hearth, of course, and was chagrined every time the media drew attention to the fact that he had been born in Liverpool. He was a good teacher and the pupils at Ysgol Ifor adored him. He was plump and he was endlessly kind to his charges and to himself. He favoured shirts in primary colours and ties hand-knitted in Bala. He was totally sincere and incurably romantic. He ate only Welsh butter and would no more have thought of reading a book in English or watching a TV programme in anything but Welsh than he would of flying to work on a broomstick. This was a genuine deprivation because he adored Westerns and it was one of the highlights of his life when one year HTV screened *Shane* with Welsh subtitles. He was a thoroughly nice man and it had caused him genuine pain to daub the second homes of holiday-makers on the Lleyn Peninsula. But at the time he had been a dedicated member of the Welsh Language Society and he had loyally obeyed the commands of the hierarchy. But after *Shane* he felt guilty every time he interfered with TV booster stations. The coming of the fourth channel with its twenty-five hours of Welsh programmes had been a blessed relief.

Meredith's dreams were in colour, shot with medieval sunshine, thronged with happy peasants enjoying *Noson Lawen*. Gareth Jenkyn dreamed in black and white, of Marxism and urban revolution. He was a small, bitter man, and curled up in sleep he looked like a twelve-year-old pyromaniac. Sleep often smooths away lines of anger bu such a liberty would have been unthinkable with Gareth Jenkyn.

Meredith, the chairman of the Red Hand of Glyndwr Society, had an uneasy feeling that Jenkyn, the society's secretary, envied him the chair. It was unfounded. Jenkyn's ambition was darker and grander.

The two had met in the Welsh Language Society in the heady days of the 'seventies when councils cringed at their bidding. Road signs had been changed, the County Regiment had been forbidden to recruit in schools and, the apogee of their campaign, the government had been forced to change its mind and set up a fourth channel for Welsh television. Perversely this, their greatest triumph, had been the mark of the Society's decline. All objectives achieved, there had been no further heights to climb. Welsh was now taught in all schools and even the smallest community councils had simultaneous translation equipment. The successful transformation of the Society into a political party and its subsequent victories in local council elections had been hollow triumphs. The idealism of the Society had been badly bruised by close contact with the earthier concerns of council. Vaguely dissatisfied, Meredith had fallen in eagerly with Gareth's suggestion that they should form a breakaway society of their own. Jenkyn realised that members would flow more readily to the popular Meredith than to himself.

Jenkyn was devoted to the cause of The People, though he did not seem to like them very much when he met them face to face. Perhaps that was why he spoke of his colleagues as card carrying members' and spent as little time in their ompany as possible. The annual rally of the Red Hand of yndwr Society was an agony to him, whereas to Meredith it s a summit of experience only previously climbed by *ne* with Welsh subtitles. Jenkyn, on the other hand, was is happiest at the Society's monthly meetings where, tly, Meredith was always slightly bored. Jenkyn got musement from setting himself monthly targets of rsion and manipulation and he achieved them with

t ps the only waking moment in which the two were

ever in accord was on Tad Day when they woke to hear on the early morning bulletin from Radiu Cymru the news of their island's declaration of independence.

Meredith could have kicked himself and Jenkyn, never selfish enough to accept blame, could have kicked him too.

From his narrow bed that morning Jenkyn reached for the phone. By the time Meredith had answered Jenkyn had decided on his posture.

'Meredith? Gareth.'

'Oh, hello,' sleepily. 'Have you heard the . . .'

'Great news, isn't it?'

'I wish we'd been informed . . .'

'Now, Meredith, we must submerge personal ambition and think only of the cause.'

'Yes, but I do think they might have consulted,' complained Meredith. Then, anxiously, for not even the highest ideals are proof against rivalry. 'You don't think they've told Plaid?'

'No, of course not. That prehistoric brute isn't interested in anyone but himself. King of the Island, boy, that's all he wants. Him and his running dog, ap Coch. What we've got to do is to work out how we can turn all this to the advantage of the proletariat.'

Meredith was always uneasy when Jenkyn talked about the proletariat. Meredith's father was a policeman and he had come to teaching via Teachers' Training at a Normal College. Jenkyn was the son of a doctor, a public schoolboy and a graduate of Cambridge.

'I don't see how we're going to do that,' Meredith said doubtfully.

'Think of the Duma, man. They served the ends of the revolution and then they were crushed.'

'But if Sir Huw didn't bother to consult us before he's hardly likely to welcome us now, is he?'

'We can still use him. Make him serve our ends.'

'I don't think that's going to be easy,' Meredith objected. He had met Sir Huw who was one of the governors of his school. But Jenkyn's plan was already formed.

'Listen,' he interrupted. 'That crazy archivist you were

talking about last week . . .'

'Miss Blair? She's not crazy. First class mind, in fact. Bit odd, perhaps, but not crazy. Eccentric, really.'

'Yes, well, anyway. You remember what you were telling me about that manuscript she'd found among the ap Gryfydd collection in the archives?'

'The Twdr letter? Yes, but the provenance is doubtful. Needs checking.'

'Never mind that. This is what I think you should do.'

Jenkyn was always careful to frame his suggestions in such a way that when he had finished Meredith was convinced that the original idea had been his and he spoke quickly for some minutes.

'Yes,' said Meredith at last, well pleased at his own perspicacity. 'What I'd better do, I think, is to ring her right away and get her to get in touch with Sir Huw.'

'You're right, of course, Mr Chairman. We should take immediate action. Whether the letter is genuine matters not. Confusion. That's what we want. Let the old boy make a fool of himself. Then we step into the vacuum of power. *Diawl*, we'll be running the whole show in a fortnight.'

Later that morning, across the island in the business room of Plas Becod, ap Gryfydd put down the phone, thought for a moment and then picked it up again.

In the lodge of Plas Coch, where he had lived since the death of his wife, ap Coch answered his call.

'Alun? Huw. Can you come to dinner?'

'Of course. Something on?'

'I've asked Miss Blair to join us.'

'Not that dreadful woman in the knitted dresses?'

'Frightful. But I think you should come. She's discovered something in those papers I gave to the archives people. Couldn't make head nor tail of it meself. But she sounded very excited.'

'She always does,' grumbled ap Coch.

'This may be different. Anyway, I think you should be here. Seven o'clock. Black tie.'

At his end of the line ap Coch's brows rose in surprise.

Black ties meant business. He knew how ap Gryfydd hated them.

'Seven o'clock, then.'

'Sharp,' said ap Gryfydd, and rang off before ap Coch, who prided himself on his punctuality, could expostulate.

By lunchtime that day every hotel on Tad was crowded with pressmen, radio reporters and TV crews arguing about their overtime. When Bob Ashton, the Welsh Affairs reporter of the *Sketch*, arrived in Byndrynkin he was lucky to find a room at the Groeslon. In fact, the room had already been taken by a rather superior young man from a Sunday paper. He had vacated it speedily when Will Looms Lloyd George heard him refer disdainfully to the soft Welsh conversation in the tap room as 'mouth knitting'.

Ashton had mixed feelings about the Groeslon. It was comfortable enough and at meal times they put on plates of food that Red Rum could not have jumped over. But Ashton, like many another before him, went in dread of the hotel's *Chef de Protocol*, an ancient chambermaid called Mary-Anne Orange.

Mary-Anne, he guessed, must have been in her eighties. She was a frail, bent woman with a face like an angry walnut. Her flowered overall was fastened with a man's belt and her freckled dome showed between the few remaining strands of her hair. As she moved she talked to herself in a Welsh of her own making. He wondered, as he did on every visit, how she came to be working at all, in apparent defiance of the Catering and Wages Act. A succession of government inspectors had wondered the same thing, aloud, to her employer.

'She won't bloody go, that's why,' Will Looms Lloyd George told them. 'I been trying to give her notice for fifteen years. She just won't take it.'

He dare not tell them that in spite of all his pleading she also insisted on arriving every morning at seven o'clock to take guests their morning tea whether they wanted it or not. She also gave them the morning papers she thought they ought to have. It mattered not at all to Mary-Anne Orange whether a man ordered *The Times*. If she thought he was a natural *Daily Mirror* man that was the paper he got.

In the bar Ashton discussed Mary-Anne with a TV presenter who had met her on the stairs and had been considerably alarmed.

'But how did she get that extraordinary nickname?' the TV man asked.

In answer Ashton called Will Looms over.

'Gentleman asking about Mary-Anne's nickname. You'd better tell him.'

He felt momentarily ashamed as he saw the slow smile play round the corner of Will's mouth. Just like a spider putting out a welcome mat for a fly, he thought.

'See,' said Will, 'she's a very independent woman, Mary-Anne. Takes a personal interest in the visitors. If she likes you, I mean really takes to you, if you see what I mean, she'll give you an orange when you're leaving. To eat on the journey home, see. Little farewell present as you leave the hotel.'

'Sounds charming,' said the TV man as Will excused himself to serve another customer.

'Think so?' said Ashton. 'Don't kid yourself. That damned witch has invented an instrument of torture that makes the thumb-screw a doddle in comparison. Never mind the lucky bugger who gets the orange. What about the poor sods that don't? I've seen holiday-makers reduced to quivering jellies wondering whether they are going to get an orange at the end of the week.

'You might think you've seen some crawlers in your business but they're selling platers compared with what I've seen here. Grown men carrying her mop and bucket for her with her cackling behind them like a gargoyle that's fallen off a church roof. Christ, they even compliment her on her disgusting tea. And I'll swear she makes it out of pan scrubbers. A fly once landed in mine and the poor little sod screamed in agony. But that's nothing,' he went on, warming to his theme. 'Do you know, there was a traveller here once made his own bed every morning and tried to borrow a vacuum cleaner to do his room?

'"What sort of a holiday did you have?"' he mimicked.

'"Oh, lovely. It rained all week but my hubby got an orange."

'I tell you, boy, it's the Tad equivalent of seaside Bingo at Rhyl.'

'I don't see what's so important about an orange,' the TV man protested.

'It's not the orange, mate. It's what it implies. It's the Tad equivalent of an Olympic Gold. If you don't get one you've somehow failed in the Game of Life. And she doesn't slip it to you quietly. Oh, no. She waits till you're at the desk paying your bill. Comes cackling out of the shadows carrying it like a bloody Mills Bomb. You can see the little queue at the desk going tense wondering who's going to get it. She only gives one, see. One a week. Cunning old sod.

'I've even seen men buying oranges at the village shop so they can flash them in the car-park. Never works. Mary-Anne's oranges are nearly as old as she is. All wrinkled and brown. They look like her, in fact. God knows what would happen if you ate one.'

'You've never had one, then?'

''Course I have,' said Ashton, untruthfully. 'Good God, what's this?'

The TV man followed his startled gaze to the lady who had just darkened the doors of the pub and who was now approaching the empty space in the bar at their side. A hastily assembled person of considerable girth at first glance she appeared to be made entirely of string. But as she came nearer the two men saw that the impression came from the assortment of cardigans she was wearing over an ankle-length knitted dress which was fighting a desperate losing battle to contain her bulk. She was carrying a briefcase and a string shopping bag bulging with documents. When she reached the bar she brought with her a faint odour of hay after rain. Ashton noticed with distaste her face powder flaked abominably and her lipstick was so carelessly applied it appeared to have been painted while her lips were in motion, as indeed they usually were.

'Evening, Miss Blair,' said John King, the barman. 'What can I get you?'

'Oh, just the teeniest gin and tonic, I think,' gushed that lady. 'I'm dining with ap Gryfydd,' she added, rather more loudly than was necessary for the benefit, it appeared, of the entire bar.

'There's nice,' said the barman with a total lack of interest, handing her the drink.

'Cheersikins!' She raised her glass to Ashton and his companions. 'Visitors to our fair isle? On holiday?' she asked.

'No,' said the TV man. 'Actually we're reporters.'

Idiot, thought Ashton savagely. Any minute now she'll be getting us to investigate the scandal over the potted honey at the WI. His fears seemed justified when she looked at them archly over the rim of her glass. Here we go, he thought, mimicking to himself: 'If I cared to open my mouth I could fill that paper of yours.'

'How very interesting,' she said. 'May I introduce myself? Blanche Magersfontein Blair. But do call me Maggie.'

Not on your bloody life, thought Ashton. She was, he judged, in her late sixties. Then he saw that the TV man, damn him, was determined to spread his professional charm.

'Do you live here or are you visiting too?'

'Gracious, no, dear man. I have a little cottage here. I came here with my sister when I retired. I was a genealogist with the College of Arms.'

'Quite a lot in your line here, I should imagine,' said Ashton, his professional curiosity reluctantly rousing. 'Very old family the ap Gryfydds, I believe.'

She tapped his arm playfully.

'You're quizzing. Naughty man. But I know what you reporters are. The man from the *Caernarvon and Denbigh Herald* pestered me most dreadfully. Alas, my lips are sealed. Quite sealed.' But she beamed at them to take the edge off their disappointment. Then she patted the briefcase she was still clutching. 'Though I could tell you a great deal . . .'

'May I get you another drink?' interrupted Ashton hastily.

She shook her head, which looked as though it had been modelled by thumb, and her impressive collection of chins applauded her resolve.

'Thank you, no. I'm bidden for seven and I see it lacks only thirty minutes to that hour. I must fly.'

'Christ, that was a near one,' said Ashton when she had left them. 'Have you no sense? Never tell anyone you're a reporter until you have to. They'll bend your ear all night.'

'Sorry,' said the TV man, muffed. 'I thought she might have recognised my face. A lot of people do, you know. It's a great trial.'

It was some time later that they learned they had missed out on the story of their lives.

What fascinated Sir Huw was the stream of recondite information which streamed from Miss Blair. With Colonel ap Coch looking ill at ease, as he invariably did in the company of lady academics, and Miss Blair behaving with the elephantine coquetry she invariably employed on him, Sir Huw settled down for an enjoyable evening.

'You mean,' he began, 'that Tad was never part of the UK at all?'

'Indeed not, Sir Huw,' she replied, whickering like a horse that has got a scent of hounds. 'No more than the Isle of Man. Or Mannan, as I prefer to call it.'

'Always thought that tourist blah,' interrupted ap Coch who scented trouble, but Miss Blair was not to be headed off.

'Very far from it, dear Colonel,' she told him. 'Very far from it, indeed.' She paused to gather breath and when she spoke again all coquetry had gone and she addressed them in quite a different tone, as academics do when they lecture. ap Coch reached despairingly for the port which she had failed to circulate.

'It's only by the merest chance that the monarch of Britain is also Lord of Man,' she began.

'Like Tad, the Isle of Man was untouched by Roman invasion and it was left to the Vikings to be both its and our first invaders. They established Mannan as a separate petty kingdom which survived until the Scottish invasion of the thirteenth century, which we were happily spared. Edward III recaptured it in 1333 and appointed the family Montacute as "Kings of Man" in perpetuity.

'Indeed, it was not until the Revesting Act of 1765 that the Lordship of Man was bought by the British parliament . . .'

'Very interesting,' said Sir Huw, to prevent a less diplomatic intervention from ap Coch who was stirring ominously. 'But I don't quite see the connection between our island and the Isle of Man.'

'Simplicity itself, dear Sir Huw,' beamed Miss Blair. 'When the Vikings landed here and fought the Battle of the Long Strand, conquering the native Gloidels, our island, like Mannan and the Shetland Isles, became part of Scandinavia. Which is why we have the Gorsedd, of course.'

The Colonel pondered for a moment, watched over his glass by a suddenly brooding Sir Huw.

'But surely,' he said at last, 'there must have been one of those, what d'ye call 'em . . .?'

'Revesting Acts.'

'Revesting Acts. Surely there must have been one of those?'

Miss Blair shook her head to the obvious alarm of her chins which shivered uncontrollably.

'Not so. The island was never invaded by the Scots, or for that matter by the Romans as Anglesey was, so it never became part of the larger political canvas.'

She paused again, her kindly washed-blue eyes shone and she delivered the phrase she had obviously polished lovingly for this moment.

'You might say that it fell through the space between the warp and the weft of history.'

'What about the Act of Union?' Sir Huw had strong feelings about the Act of Union which had robbed Wales of her independence. A lot of his neighbouring squires' ancestors had moved to London and made their fortunes. Often at the expense of those, like the ap Gryfydds, who had stayed at home.

Miss Blair beamed happily.

'It was assumed that the island was part of Wales. But, as I have shown, it's not and it never has been.'

Both men were now hanging on her words and their reaction delighted Miss Blair who threw her hands in the air, waggling every one of her chins, and what was more alarming, her extravagant bosom began to move majestically in unison.

'But there is more, much more. Not only is this island a separate kingdom. It belongs, dear Sir Huw, to you.'

Sir Huw had been hypnotised by the movements of Miss Blair's bosom which resembled a monstrous land-slip, but the suggestion that something that belonged to the ap Gryfydds had been kept from his family for half a millenium concentrated his attention at once.

'How d'ye mean?' he demanded.

With another cry of triumph Miss Blair delved in turn into the pockets of each of her several cardigans, found at last a key, and with it opened the briefcase which lay at her feet. She brought out a large pocket-book with an embroidered cover depicting violets and from it extracted a torn sheet of parchment which she laid on the table and covered from Sir Huw's avaricious gaze with her hand.

'Your family were followers of Richard II, I believe, and that generous king bestowed on them rights similar to those bestowed on the earls of Chester in Cheshire.'

Sir Huw nodded, still glaring at the parchment.

'But, unlike the earls, they retained their lands throughout the turbulent years that followed. Finally they gave gallant support to the Earl of Richmond, later to become Henry VII . . .'

'Yes, yes, and then that damned son of his brought in the Act of Union.'

'Not applicable, as I have demonstrated,' Miss Blair told him. 'Especially with the evidence I have here.'

And she tapped the parchment. ap Coch intervened hurriedly, sensing that his friend and chieftain was at bursting point.

'And may we know what that evidence is?'

'Certainly,' cried Miss Blair triumphantly. 'Some time ago Sir Huw was kind enough to present the contents of his muniment room to the island and, as you know, they are now housed at the library in Byndrynkin. I've spent many happy hours there browsing among the old papers and I've made many small finds which have quite excited. You may have seen my occasional contributions on the subject in the Caernarvon and Denbigh *Herald*.'

Both men agreed untruthfully that they had.

'But you will have seen nothing of this,' she said, tapping the parchment. 'Despite the persistent importunings of their district correspondent, a very able lady, a Mrs Brownson, perhaps you know her . . .?'

'For God's sake, woman, what is it?' roared Sir Huw.

Miss Blair waved an admonitory finger at the chieftain. 'Patience, Sir Huw. Firstly its provenance. I found it between the sheepskin membranes of some Manorial Court Rolls which, due to the damp condition of your muniment room – such a mistake not to have it heated – had become stuck together and, I judge, had been so for some four hundred years . . .'

'The parchment, Miss Blair!'

'. . . which, to my mind, proves at least its age . . .'

'But WHAT IS IT?'

'It's a letter, or rather part of a letter addressed to your ancestor, Llewellyn ap Gryfydd.'

'That's Henry Seven's old chum.'

'Exactly, Sir Huw. And now, if I may, I will read it.'

Another search in her pocket to fish out a pair of spectacles with adhesive tape binding the bridge and enormous lenses. Clearing her throat and humming quietly to herself she studied the document and at last began to read.

'It's addressed to Sir Llewellyn and the first lines are, I'm afraid, lost. The damp, you know. But it begins . . . "that you doe keep these islanders in thrifty governance and doe always to the kings purpose in time of war shall you be confirmed in those ancient rights that were yours by Plantagenet hand. Let this be privie until . . ." and then, I'm afraid, the damp has once again obliterated the rest.'

'Is that all?' asked Colonel ap Coch, disappointed.

'It's rather more than you think,' Miss Blair told him. 'Of course, when I found the document I at once appraised the committee of the Tad Historical Society. Indeed, it was our worthy secretary, Mr Meredith ap Owen, who suggested I bring it to your attention. Unfortunately he was in rather a hurry when he rang me this morning and I was not able to tell him of the most recent development.'

'Really,' the Colonel thought, 'it's like unravelling her damned knitted frock.' The picture conjured up was so bizarre he hurled it from his mind.

'And that is?' he asked.

'I have a chum who is a Consultant Graphologist to the College of Arms. And I'm afraid I rather jumped the gun and sent it to her to test my theory.'

'Which was?'

'Simply that it might have been written by Henry VII when he was Earl of Richmond. The membrane dates would be about right. It was probably hidden in case his rebellion failed.'

'And was it?'

'My friend returned it this morning with her report. Would you like to see it?'

'Summarise it, madam, for God's sake,' growled Sir Huw.

'As you may know, the law requires seventeen points of similarity for such identifications. This letter contains twenty-four. Undoubtedly, therefore, it amply satisfies the required criteria and was written by Henry VII.'

'But that means . . .' the Colonel began.

'Exactly,' said Miss Blair turning to Sir Huw. 'That means – since your family were out with the Earl of Richmond and thus fulfilled the terms of the agreement – that your family are undoubtedly Kings of Tad.'

'But the Act of Union?' Sir Huw persisted.

'Does not apply to Tad. How can it? The island was no longer part of the kingdom. Henry VIII couldn't include something his father had given over in return for military aid.'

'D'you mean what we're doing is quite legal?' burst out the Colonel.

'Absolutely,' rejoined Miss Blair, 'though, of course, you would have to establish your right in the courts.'

'Which courts?' asked Sir Huw.

'The international courts, I rather think.'

'European Court of Human Rights?' This from ap Coch.

'I should think that would be the proper channel. Though expensive.'

'Worth every blasted penny,' sighed Sir Huw contentedly. 'My dear Miss Blair! Do have another glass of port.'

At just about the same time in the darkened bar of the Groeslon, Bob Ashton was being offered a last drink by the man from the *Telegraph*.

'Much doing?' the *Telegraph* man asked.

'Nothing hard,' Ashton told him. 'I filed a nice colour piece earlier. Tell me, what do you think of that TV chap, Johnson?'

'All right, I think. Why?'

'Bloody fool nearly ruined my evening. Got us tied up with some crazy old bat of a genealogist. Told her we were reporters. I thought we'd be stuck with her all night.'

'Some people never learn,' said the *Telegraph* man sagely.

'Too right,' said Ashton.

Some time later the telephone rang across the road in Gareth Jenkyn's flat over the Oxfam shop.

'Gareth? Meredith. Tried to get you earlier. Thought I'd let you know my little idea worked out perfectly. She's having dinner with Huw Know Who.'

'She fell for it, then?'

'Hook, Line and Sinker. She was so keen I had to cut her off in mid-sentence.'

'Bloody marvellous.'

'Good night, then.'

'Good night.'

And they both went to bed to dream about revolutions.

CHAPTER SIX

'My dear Field Marshall, don't talk rubbish.' It had been a hard day and the Prime Minister's patience was wearing thin. 'We cannot invade Tad.'

'On the contrary, Prime Minister,' Field Marshal Sir Franklyn Cloudesley-Shovel, Chief of the Defence Staff committee, contradicted, 'we have the capability and my committee has prepared a feasibility study that shows a choice of four assault beaches . . .'

'Field Marshal. Please. Listen to me.' The Prime Minister broke in with a weary grip on fast failing patience. 'We don't do it like that any more. You've not, I think, been with us very long?'

'No, Prime Minister. As you know, I was with the Pentagon until my appointment last month.'

'Of course, Reagan's Invincibles,' said the PM as though that explained everything. 'But, d'you see, our strategy is quite other than that of our American cousins. It's been so long since we could afford to invade anywhere we've learned to operate differently. Our wars are fought in newspapers and on TV bulletins. Learned it at Suez, really. Profit by your mistakes. Suez, d'ye see, was the first of the newspaper wars. We lost it, of course, but, by God, we learned from it. May I explain?'

'Please do,' acknowledged the Field Marshal huffily.

'Now, supposing we wanted to invade France . . .'

'Not before time,' growled the Field Marshal. 'Sorry . . .'

'Thank you. Now, what we'd do would be to have a – what do you call it? Landing in force, that's it. Say at Dunkirk. Something emotional, d'you see, for our people. Right? That night TV bulletins are full of it. Pictures next day in every paper. Frighten the hell out of Frogs. America steps in. Requests cease fire while the Security Council discuss it. Peace keeping force sent in. We argue the toss a bit. Make angry noises. Then, like English gentlemen, we go back to our corner. We make an outrageous demand. France rejects it, which means that they've got to demonstrate their Gallic gallantry by making some concession. And that's when we bring out the demand for the lesser thing that we really wanted in the first place.

'These days, Field Marshal, we fight all our wars in the newspapers. It's a lot cheaper and no one gets hurt. But it's a matter of fine judgment. Can you imagine just what sort of a press I'd get if I let you play John Wayne on the beach at Aberbrigant? It's hardly Iwojima and at this time of year you wouldn't be able to deploy your troops for holiday-makers. English holiday-makers. And most of them, I may add, of voting age. It would be disastrous. Can you see that sort of invasion on the front pages? I'd be a laughing stock all over the world. Do have some sense, man.'

The PM waved aside the soldier's stiff protest. 'I'm sorry. Cares of office. Forgive me. But you do see, don't you, invasion on the lines you advise is out of the question?'

The Field Marshal nodded sulkily.

'But what are we going to do?'

'What we are going to do is what we always do. We're going to form a committee. It will be called the Tad Committee and it will meet under the chairmanship of the Secretary of State for Wales. I hope you, Field Marshal, will consent to serve under him as military adviser? I know he will want to have the benefit of your valuable experience.'

The Field Marshal nodded, mollified.

'Good. It's going to cost us money whatever happens so we'd better have the Treasury represented. Oh, and the TUC, of course.'

'Don't see what it's got to do with the Unions,' the Field Marshal protested.

'My dear Field Marshal, you have been away a long time. If the Unions concerned themselves only with things that had got to do with Unions this country would be a lot easier to govern.'

The PM turned to the Secretary of State for Wales who had wisely let the Field Marshal ask all the silly questions he would otherwise have put himself.

'Clear, Gwilym? Good.'

Standing up the Prime Minister drew the rest of the people in the room to their feet.

'I don't think we can usefully take this matter further. You'll report your conclusions directly to me, of course. And we'll act upon your wise counsels.'

When it came to passing the buck no one had seen the PM's like in Britain since the days of Robin Hood and his band of venison poachers.

Colonel ap Coch had been on the mainland for what he hoped would be the final visit to his specialist in Chester. Surprisingly, though he supposed technically he was behind enemy lines, no one had attempted to detain him as he thought they might. His specialist had approved thoroughly of independence and even suggested that he might come up and set up a practice on Tad, and the policeman at Port Penrhyn, where he boarded the ferry, had saluted him with a broad smile and a wink.

All the same he was glad to be aboard the *Queen of Tad* and half way across the strait. His mood lightened as it always did when he had put the mainland behind him.

The feeling of escape was heightened by an unconscious conspiracy of architecture. On the mainland the landscape was dominated by a Victorian sham Gothic castle, built by a quarry master and towering over the mean rows of dark granite houses where his quarrymen had lived.

In contrast the goose pie of cottages which ran down to the shore on the island were, for the most part, pink-washed or glistening white, with, here and there, others painted in dove-grey, light blue and yellow. As he did every time he approached the island the Colonel blessed the kindly providence that had arranged for him to be born there.

Chance acquaintances found the Colonel aloof. Those who knew him loved him for his warmth and humanity. Those who had been brushed by his icy good manners did not. It was the Colonel's motor car which gave the clue to his inner self. He drove a white MG TD and though he viewed the internal combustion engine with great suspicion he loved his car. It was the last of a long line of treasured MGs. He had found it ten years before in a barn on the island covered with fowl droppings, its engine missing. But the sight of it brought back such happy memories of the 'fifties that he had bought it at once and spent what he described as a 'handsome sum' on its restoration. It was waiting for him on the quayside. He climbed in gratefully and as he turned off the jetty and drove along the cliff road to his club the engine growled in perfect tune.

The Yacht Club on the banks of a small estuary had been in turn an Edwardian villa, a mess for the pilots of a wartime seaplane squadron, and was now a sailing club.

It stood a little below the moorings where the seaplanes had ridden the swell like monstrous sea birds, but the planes had gone now and the pilots too. Even the estuary was silted up and a new Marine Drive had replaced the old road which had run past the club. The dining-room and the elegant lounges had been converted into holiday flats and now only the bar remained of its past elegance with above it the club badge, a ship sinking over its motto *In Vino Veritas*.

For all that it was a cheerful bar with a membership that had just the right mixture of casual friendliness that the Colonel enjoyed. He had christened his cronies the 'Government of All the Talents'. It was an apt name. They were, for the most part, Tad-born men and women who had enjoyed distinguished careers on the mainland and hurried home the day that they retired or had been made redundant. They represented an impressive array of commercial, professional and technical talent.

He ordered a brandy and soda and carried it out to a balcony where a group was idly watching a heron fishing in the shallows. They greeted him with an ironic cheer and one whistled the opening bars of 'Hail, the Conquering Hero'. It was his first visit to the club since UDI and he was apprehensive about the reaction of his friends. He need not have worried. They were all whole-heartedly in favour. Though a particular chum, another ex-Marine, Tom Fort, had a warning.

'I'm afraid you're in the Galloping Major's bad books.

He's furious you didn't call on his terriers.'

'Good God,' said the Colonel, striking his forehead with the heel of his hand. 'I forgot all about him.'

'Oh dear,' grinned Tom, 'don't ever let him hear you say that.'

Major David Tufton-Bellis had commanded the island's TA unit and he had been furious when it had been disbanded as an economy measure. For nearly four years it had continued to parade and train as a voluntary body, only to disband at last with great reluctance at the express command of the Army Council.

But for all that, the Colonel remembered, they were a useful, spirited lot. The islanders call them 'Tufton-Bellis's Terriers' but never to their faces. They were mainly fishermen and farm workers, ex-commandos, paratroops, even a small group of SAS men. He made a note to contact the Major and then turned to sound the opinions of the group on the takeover of the island.

'Well, frankly,' said Tom, 'I don't think you've begun to explore the possibilities.'

The Colonel listened attentively. Tom had built up a large business on the mainland and was said to be approaching millionaire status. Then he had come home for a sailing holiday. On the last day the thought of returning to the world of business had so appalled him that on impulse he had telephoned his resignation to his board, bought a small villa on a headland and had never crossed to the mainland since. But he had a shrewd business brain.

'We've opened negotiations with the oil company about getting the toll paid to us,' ap Coch told him. 'But, frankly, I know little of business and I'd be glad of a briefing.'

'Well, there's offshore banking, for a start. Even casinos, but I don't suppose ap Gryfydd would care for that.'

'Nor should I,' said the Colonel quickly. 'Attract quite the wrong element.'

'What I would suggest is something much wider. But why don't you tap the brains in this club? Look at us. Successful businessmen, lawyers, engineers, bankers, retired servicemen, even civil servants. Turned out to grass, most of them, just because their bodies have reached the age of sixty. But what about their brains? Brains last longer than bodies and they store the experience of a lifetime. Central government has a think tank, why don't you? You couldn't buy an assembly of better brains than you'll find in this club. I've often thought what a criminal waste it all is. Good God, a man's just finding what it's all about when he's sixty. And what do they do? They dump him and let all that acumen run to waste.'

'It's a wonderful idea. But do you think they'd want to be bothered?'

'Bothered? They'd bite your hand off. Bored to death, most of them. Youngsters make jokes about old men sitting back, solving the problems of the world. The irony is that they can, if only they're given the chance. And not only the high-powered lads. What about all the old craftsmen who've been turned out to grass. Dammit, d'you know, there are only five watchmakers in the country who can repair a decent watch. Disposable society. If it's a couple of years old, chuck it away, that's the business philosophy over there!' And he waved his hand towards the mainland. 'And chuck the craftsmen away too. Believe me, you'd be doing them a favour. Look, would you like me to sound a few of them out?'

The Colonel emptied his glass and got up to go.

'By God, I would,' he said. 'Y'know I was dead against this UDI thing at first. Thought it was another bit of ap Gryfydd's nonsense. But, damme, I feel twenty years younger already.'

'And you look it, too,' Tom told him. 'Leave it with me. I'll take soundings and report back.'

Driving home the Colonel was well pleased with his visit. Government of All the Talents, he thought. Many a true word . . .

Before supper that evening he took his gin into the garden at the back of his lodge. Once in the prison camp, living like an animal on rice husks and water and stews made from the offal of jungle pigs, he had promised himself that if he ever got out he would make himself a garden like the one in which he now walked. When he came back after the war the garden at the back of the lodge had been a tangle of brambles and the rubble of demolished out-buildings. Yard by yard he and his wife had won it back. It had taken them three years, but it had been fun. They'd always planned to move out of the big house when they were old, for they had no children. And then she had died and there had only been the garden. If only she could see it now. Ah well, he'd be seeing her soon and he could tell her. He looked with pride at the ranks of vegetables and beyond them the small orchard. He wasn't rich. He had his pension and the income from a few shares. He'd sold the big house at the wrong time, of course, but there was a bit left. I'm a lucky devil, he thought, and I really don't want to stay much longer. Things were in a hell of a mess on the mainland. Everywhere except here, on Tad. His soldier's instinct told him that the clouds of yet another war were gathering. True, they were only wisps on the horizon, but they were there. He recognised the signs. He'd seen them before in the 'thirties. It was different now, of course. No place for his kind of soldiering. The next war would be a scientist's battle. He looked beyond the garden to the garage where he could see the outline of his old MG. It brought back memories; adventures, scrapes and fears. How wonderful to be young then, driving the first of that series of cars; embarking on a madcap jaunt! He grinned suddenly. Madcap jaunt? There could scarcely be anything more madcap than hijacking an island.

'I must go in and ring the Galloping Major,' he thought. 'Mustn't keep all the fun to myself.'

CHAPTER SEVEN

Major David Tufton-Bellis attracted nicknames. He was the Galloping Major to his friends, a reference to his air of frenzied bustle, and Dai Double-Time to the soldiers of his TA unit for much the same reason. He was a small cannon ball of a man with a brisk little moustache and he went everywhere at a brisk little trot. He had brisk little eyes that stared out of his brisk little face and darted about questing for idleness. Major Tufton-Bellis abhorred idleness. His origins were humble, but in the days before the war whilst working in a bank in Swansea, he had joined the TA. In 1939 he had been commissioned into a good infantry regiment. Quickly taking on the colouring of the public school men he met in the mess he had become, over the years, almost indistinguishable from the genuine article.

Over the years Tufton-Bellis (the Tufton was really a second Christian name) had disguised his origins with a skill which in the theatre would have earned him a peerage. He was socially a quick read. But it was still an act and needed his constant attention. There were a thousand tricks of pronunciation, quirks of dress and nuances of behaviour lying in wait to betray him. In his young manhood he had taken them in his stride. He had been very good at copying those mannerisms of the stars. He could shoot a cuff with Niven, exhibit the social gallantry of Granger. But he had been younger then and slimmer. As he grew older the act had slipped into caricature. His conversation was just too heavily loaded with 'bidden to dines' and 'four-letter men'. He talked of his 'bluff soldier's manner' to excuse the frequent rudenesses which the strain of keeping up the act induced. And the sensitive winced when he spoke of 'the lower classes' being 'basically sound'.

The irony was that none of it was necessary. Men like the Colonel knew all about his background and thought it unimportant. They tolerated his self-caricature because they knew he had been a very brave soldier. His MC had been well deserved. They also took every advantage of his willingness to run their errands or carry out tiresome chores. The Major would have been bitterly unhappy if he had known that these were the reasons his name had been put forward in the first place to command the island's Home Guard. He would never realise, poor man, that being an officer and a gentleman isn't always the same thing. And now he had let himself in for the most embarrassing chore of all.

A connoisseur of character might have been able to identify the separate ingredients which merged in his personality. There was something in him from almost every star of the wartime cinema battle epics. He favoured black barathea blazers, bright with gold buttons bearing the crest of his regiment, though not, of course, a badge on the breast pocket which was the sign of an Other Rank. The crest appeared again on his cuff-links and he always wore a regimental tie. His shoes were as black and twinkling as a diddicoy's eye. His other uniform was a suit of screaming tweeds in which he looked dreadful; chukka boots and, of course, his regimental tie. He disguised his natural timidity with a gruff, prickly manner. An internal turbulence which this social schizophrenia provoked murmured perpetually in his breast and when, as he frequently did, he drowned it with whisky he became aggressive and hectoring. His wartime experience made him the natural choice. If his men did not love him, as he deluded himself they did, at least they accepted him with affectionate tolerance.

He lived with his wife, whom, inevitably, he referred to as the 'Memsahib', in a charming regency cottage on the outskirts of Byndrynkin. And that admirable lady accepted the soubriquet with the tolerance with which she regarded most of his little poses.

When he replaced the phone after the Colonel's call he walked thoughtfully back to the sitting-room where his wife was pouring the pre-dinner sherry.

'Anything important, darling?'

'It's the Call. I was rather expecting it. Surprised they didn't alert me earlier.'

'The call, dear? I know. I heard the bell. I was wondering who it was who was ringing.'

He gave her a look of exasperation.

'ap Coch. Wants to see me. Tomorrow. 11 ack emma. I'll take the mini.'

'Yes, dear. Will you be home to lunch?'

'Lunch? 'Course I shall. Why ever not?'

Mealtimes had taken the place of parades in his fantasy life and the idea that he should miss one, or even be late, was a heresy.

'Just a chat and a talk. Back in minutes thirty.'

But the next day the gallant major was not back in minutes thirty. Indeed, so late was he that the luncheon liver had been twice reheated and looked like a sun-baked scrotum by the time the Major returned to eat it. So overcooked was it that Madge Tufton-Bellis was nervous about offering it, for the Major was very particular about his food. To her amazement he ate it with no comment at all. Clearly whatever the Colonel wanted her husband for had been very important indeed. As they sat down she asked:

'Did you have a nice chat, dear? What did Alun want?'

She was startled to see a quick spasm of apprehension draw itself across her husband's lightly boiled eyes.

'Nothing at all. Nothing at all. Worried about his strawberries.'

'In August, dear?'

It was said innocently enough but in his mind's eye the Major saw the flashing messages, 'Walls Have Ears', 'Careless Talk Costs Lives'.

'Why not in August?' he demanded crossly.

'Hardly the season, is it?'

'I think ap Coch has gone mad,' the Major burst out at last, no longer able to contain himself. 'I think we all have.'

'Yes, dear,' his wife agreed.

It had been her opinion for years. She asked no further questions but her long marriage had made her an expert tracker. She could read signs which were more eloquent than speech. And when presently the Major went to sit in his greenhouse she knew that something was UP.

He only ever took a deck-chair into the greenhouse when he was deeply troubled, she knew. The steaming heat took him back to his wartime service in the jungles of Burma and was oddly consoling. Surrounded by glass on all sides, no one could approach without him seeing them and there was no danger of eavesdroppers. He could confide in his cucumbers in total security. He did so now.

'We'll all go to prison,' he told them sadly. 'Sure as eggs.'

He had agreed at once when ap Coch had asked him to remuster his territorial platoon as Tad's Standing Army. He had done so once before during the Russian invasion threat of 1982. When men like the Colonel commanded, men like the Major obeyed.

When he had heard of the plan to seize the island he had gone into his sabre-rattling role by Pavlovian response. He had been 'ready to answer the call', publicly distressed that ap Gryfydd, who could not stand him and would never make use of him at any price, had not called on his services. But, secretly, he had been deeply relieved. It was not that he was afraid of battle, but he lived in mortal fear of humiliation. It had stood too long a spectre at his elbow. And it seemed to him this adventure was bound to end in arrest and disgrace. He saw himself being dragged to the Tower of London, relieved of his commission and stripped of his Military Cross. The whole thing would be published in the *London Gazette*, like as not.

But, as always, Colonel ap Coch won him over with a careful cocktail of flattery and brusque command.

Thank goodness, he thought as he sat in his greenhouse, they had no ammunition. It had all gone back to Ordnance when the '82 Russian scare blew over. Fortunately the Colonel had been adamant that there was to be no gun play.

'We don't want anybody hurt,' he reassured the Major. 'At least not BADLY hurt.'

But supposing they had to attack the police? Superintendent Jones's police. Like all ex-rankers the Major had never overcome his terror of Regimental Sergeant Majors. And attacking the police after all he'd said about football hooligans? It was too horrible to contemplate.

From the kitchen where she was watching him Madge saw the poor Major shake his head slowly at his plants. He was still shaking it as he walked out of the greenhouse. And then he did something so uncharacteristic Madge thought she was hallucinating. She called to him from the kitchen.

'David! David, dear! You've left the greenhouse door open and it's rather chilly . . .'

The Major looked at her for a long time across the crew-cut lawn.

'Oh, bugger the greenhouse,' he wailed. 'I'm going to the Groeslon.'

Alas, as he marched down the lane, flicking at the autumn fruits with his cane, he knew there would be an indifferent welcome awaiting him there. If he had never quite joined the class to which he had aspired, the effort had lost him the sympathy of the class into which he had been born. The Major was a very lonely man. He would have given anything at that moment for the rough goodwill of the tap room. ap Gryfydd would have sought it instantly, ap Coch would have merged effortlessly. But to Major Tufton-Bellis it was Terra Incognita. It would have meant Loss of Face.

When he reached the pub he saw, to his dismay, that McCafferty, the Irishman who had been his platoon sergeant in the TA, was talking to Superintendent Jones, the central character in his recent nightmare.

'Jaysis,' said McCafferty *sotto voce* when he in turn saw the Major. 'It's bloody Dai Double-Time. This is going to cost me a Scotch. That feller'd have the knickers off a nun.'

'Didn't know they wore 'em,' replied the Superintendent, who managed to be both chapel and coarse.

'Now ye grasp the magnitude of the problem.'

'Don't worry, he'll never come in the vault with the peasants,' the Superintendent reassured him.

It was true, usually, but the Major desperately wanted to pass on ap Coch's instructions to his platoon sergeant. At first he tried to convey this by a series of brisk upwards and sideways movements of his head from the door of the snug whenever he caught McCafferty's eye. Out of perversity

McCafferty at first ignored these cranial jerks, then he pretended to see them as a nod of greeting, which he returned. The Major was no match for McCafferty and at last he was forced to surrender and step inside the snug.

'Mr McCafferty,' he called, 'may I have a word with you?'

If he had hoped that this would bring McCafferty to his side he was to be disappointed. McCafferty was too great an expert in pub psychology. He knew that the one who moves first loses.

'Of course, Major, darlin',' he called, winning the bout with a single move. 'Come in, come in. Sure you're as welcome as the flowers, the very flowers . . .'

Seething with baffled rage the defeated Major gave in, and pushing his way through the customers, joined the two men at the bar.

'Evenin' Superintendent,' he began nervously.

'Evening Major,' rejoined the Superintendent with a knowing smile. 'And a lovely evening for the UDI, *chwarae teg*.'

'Good God!' The Major could not hide his astonishment. 'You're in favour of it, then?'

'Bless you, Major *bach*. Why ever not? They're breaking no law that I can see. Just a change in administration as the result of a resolution properly voted by local government. It's the duty of my small force to uphold the administration, surely?'

In fact the Superintendent had just that morning sounded out his superiors in Colwyn Bay and had been told to play it by ear. He was glad. His sympathies were wholly with ap Gryfydd, but he was a career policeman and he had already laid contingency plans for arresting the leaders should that be ordered by HQ at Colwyn Bay.

'I've had a long talk with Sir Huw,' he told the Major. 'He has assured me there will be no gratuitous violence. And I have had no complaints from anyone. With the help of your TA unit, which I understand you have very kindly agreed to re-muster to assist me, I'm sure that we can effectively contain the situation and prevent anything untoward?'

The Major's relief was comic and it did not escape his

companions who had been effortlessly reading his mind. The shadow of the Tower had lifted from his soul.

'Can I buy you chaps a drink?' he asked, an unusual thing in itself. He even attempted a small face-saving joke. 'If it's permitted in your Mess, of course.'

'Well now, Major,' McCafferty said, 'that's very kind of you. And to celebrate the historic moment I'll just take a large Scotch.'

'Stirring times, right enough,' the Superintendent agreed. 'May I have the same?'

'Yes, indeed,' said the Major weakly. 'Landlord!'

Will Looms Lloyd George, who hated anyone calling him landlord, took the Major's money with savage pleasure. The Major accepted his change, put it in a leather purse and returned the purse to an inner pocket of his jacket which he buttoned carefully. Clearly there was going to be no repetition of his largesse that evening.

'How do the chaps feel about it?' he asked McCafferty.

'Behind you to a man,' replied McCafferty, raising his whisky glass in salute. 'Your very good health, Major.'

Gravely the Superintendent raised his glass.

'To a peaceful occupation, sir.'

'Indeed, indeed,' the Major replied, more relieved than he could remember ever feeling. What jolly good chaps they were, to be sure. Salt of the Earth.

He would have been less relieved could he have heard a conversation which was going on at that moment in the more sedate surroundings of the office of the Secretary of State for Wales, Gwilym Meredith-Evans. He had just dropped a bombshell and Field Marshal Sir Franklyn Cloudesley-Shovel was piqued.

'Policemen, Secretary of State? A landing in force by policemen? It's so dashed unfair. They get all the fun. I remember when if a chap wanted to see the world he joined the services. Now he's better off in the Metropolitan Police. D'you realise there are inspectors of police with more campaign medals than my infantry commanders? Wonder to me the blighters can remember how to direct traffic.'

'Special Patrol Group, of course,' Meredith-Evans hurried to soothe him. 'Hand-picked chaps.'

The Field Marshal was not to be soothed.

'Hand-picked for every decent show that offers itself. Some of my chaps go further on leave than they do on active service.'

The Secretary of State raised a hand in friendly but unmistakable warning.

'The PM is adamant, I fear. No soldiers. We're even using Sea Cadets to ferry them across the strait in inflatables.'

'Good God!' The soldier was shocked. 'The First Sea Lord will be livid. He's still bitterly unhappy about the Cabinet's decision to lease Plymouth dockyard to that firm of Japanese shipbuilders.'

Again the warning hand.

'Cabinet decision, Field Marshal. And they do repair all our ships at a special price. Forward planning, forward thinking. Government of Vision, my dear fellow. But we stray. I'm afraid there is no question of using your chaps. Surely you see one simply cannot invade one's own country? We should look such frightful fools in the eyes of the world.'

'Yes, so the PM explained,' the Field Marshal conceded. 'Personally I can't think why you don't give them Home Rule.'

'Good God, man,' snapped the Secretary of State, 'do you think we haven't tried? It would have saved us a fortune and we'd have had none of that frightful unemployment in the first half of this decade laid at our door. Dammit, people wouldn't have it. That was the trouble.'

'Can't we even be Beach Masters?' pleaded the Field Marshal.

The Secretary of State shook his head.

'I truly am sorry,' he said. 'A.A., I'm afraid. PM's a member and we get their services free.'

It was the final humiliation. The Field Marshal got out of his chair, excused himself and returned to the security of his own office at Horse Guards. And there, among the brass and mahogany and the leather chairs, Field Marshal Sir Franklyn Cloudesley-Shovel sought his own way of release. Crossing from his desk he took a key from his ring, opened a cupboard and gazed at a scene of pageantry such as he would never see again on the parade ground outside his window, leased now to the National Car Parks Organisation.

On the shelves, drawn up in their ranks, was his collection of model soldiers. There were guardsmen, kilted infantrymen and native levies, frozen at the march: squadrons of cavalry caught in a canter. There was a troop of the Camel Corps; Indian troops in the glorious uniforms of the Raj; the King's Troop of the RHA with their horse teams and limbers. There were Royal Marine bands in navy uniforms and white pith helmets, Pipe Bands in the Royal Stuart tartan, and the green kilts of the Ulster Regiment. The Field Marshal took out one of the marching guardsmen and held it in the palm of his hand. There were tears in his eyes. He looked from it to the massed ranks of its fellows on the shelves.

'I've got more soldiers in the damned cupboard than I've got under arms,' he told himself. 'And they've seen nearly as much action, too.'

Over the years the role of the British Army had diminished. The decision by Eire and Ulster to become the fifty-first State of America had removed the last battle ground. Now a chap couldn't even go to war in his own country.

A knock on his door disturbed him. Hastily he replaced the soldier, locked the cupboard and scurried back to his desk, removing the service cap which he always wore when he was reviewing his toy soldiers.

'COME!' he roared, himself again.

His ADC came in carrying his list of the next day's engagements.

'Any luck about Tad, sir?' he asked.

''fraid not. Those darned bobbies again.'

'Oh, bad show, sir. I know how much you were looking forward to it. It really is too bad.'

'Yes, my boy. And even worse if it's successful. Never be able to hold our face up again. Might just as well chuck.'

'Couldn't we leak it, sir? Know an awfully nice *Guardian*

chappie. Man called Whewell. Wykehamist, I believe. Very sound.'

The Field Marshal shook his head.

'Won't do, I'm afraid. Remember that terrible fuss over the estimates in '80? We'd both be bowler hatted. I'd finish my career yarning with a bunch of old biddies in some seaside hotel.' He paused. 'Yarning with old biddies . . . just a minute . . .'

An idea was forming. It was unworthy but it was a pippin. He wrestled with his conscience and was rather surprised how quickly it was overcome. 'Shut the door, Piers,' he said, and the ADC did so. 'From the army's point of view a police victory would be a disaster. Our future role would be jeopardised. Agreed?'

'Yes, sir.'

'Well then, we must pray for opposition. In the National Interest, of course,' he added quickly.

'Of course, sir.'

'Sort of thing only a trained soldier could be expected to handle. They'd have to come back to the army then.'

'Yes, sir.'

'So what it comes to is this. Someone has got to remove the element of surprise. In the National Interest, of course.'

Yes, indeed, thought the Field Marshal. But, of course, it must never be traced back to him. He beamed at the ADC. 'You're Welsh, are you not?'

'Yes, sir. Matter of fact this ap Gryfydd's a sort of uncle. Not seen him since I was a child, of course.'

'Any leave coming?'

'Leave, sir? 'fraid not.'

'Then we must arrange some. Don't want your people to think we're slave-drivers, eh? And talkin' about one's people, I do sometimes think that one's loved ones don't quite appreciate the sort of thing we soldiers have to put up with from these damned politicals. Did I understand you to say you were related to ap Gryfydd?'

'Yes, sir, through the Mater, actually.'

'Mater, eh? What do you think she'd think if she knew

we'd been usurped by those damned flat-feet in their pointed helmets?'

'Absolutely furious, sir. She's from an army family.'

'Really? She'd be pretty upset, I imagine, if she ever found out these politicians plan to keep us twiddling our thumbs on November 11 while they send forty damned policemen across the straits in inflatables. Inflatables, crewed, if you please, by bally Sea Cadets!'

'I think it would go round the family like wild fire, sir.'

'Really? Pity, really, that the Official Secrets Act forbids you to tell her. Odd business, that. I never did like keeping secrets from my family. After all, they're the ones who suffer most from army life, I always feel. Ah well, mustn't keep you jawing here all day. Work to do. Bring your pass in to me tonight and I'll sign it. Forty-eight hours enough?'

'Oh, thank you, sir. Cubbing started last week. Nice to have a day and I'll see most of the family.'

'Good. Good. Do tell your Mama we were talking about her.'

'Oh yes, sir,' said the ADC, to whom a nod was every bit as good as a wink. 'I won't forget.'

Left alone the Field Marshal stamped down feelings of shame. After all, the islanders weren't really an enemy. Damn it, they were British. He sought consolation at his cupboard, but he found none. It seemed that every little painted face was glaring at him with disapproval. He shut the door hurriedly and went back to his desk. Try as he would not to he kept thinking about Lord Raglan and the Russian deserter. The Russian had offered to supply Lord Raglan with the the Russian troop deployments on the Crimea. Lord Raglan had refused to listen and admonished the boy. 'What would your mothing think of you?' he had said.

That day, for the first time since he had taken up his appointment the Field Marshal did not lunch at the 'In and Out'.

CHAPTER EIGHT

'Policemen?' bellowed ap Gryfydd down the phone. 'Blasted Peelers? Island overrun with PC Plods? Handin' out parking tickets and thrusting those nasty unhygienic bag things down the throats of perfectly respectable people?'

An obviously exasperated voice on the end of the line elaborated in a whisper.

'London policemen?' It was worse than he had thought. 'God! I'd almost rather have the Yanks back. You're sure?'

Indignant whispering now.

'Alice's boy? Do I know him? Oh yes, I remember. Sneaky sort of brute with teeth. Face looked as though it was being held together by acne. That the one?'

Even more indignant whispering; the muffled cry of an affronted aunt. ap Gryfydd was contrite.

'Yes, yes. Sorry. Charming boy, I'm sure. Must bring him over some time for a spot of fishing. Yes, I'm sure he's changed greatly. Not seen him since his school days, of course. I'm bound to say that in those days the acne was cropping several bushels to the acre. Still. Very good of him to let you know. And of you, too, of course. My daughter Ceri? Oh, still in London. Yes, do. Goodbye.'

The phone replaced, ap Gryfydd thought for a moment before picking it up again.

'Damned policemen. Well, we'll show them. Truncheons, notebooks, breath bags and all.'

He rang ap Coch first, then certain friends among whom was the owner of Tad Flying Club and Captain Bill, a straits pilot, and to each he gave precise instructions. Then he set off on a delicate diplomatic mission to Superintendent Idris Jones.

When, in his turn, ap Coch telephoned Major Tufton-Bellis that unfortunate man could only gabble ineffectually. Once again he saw the grim outline of Traitors Gate and the portcullis opening to swallow him for ever.

‘Policemen?’ he gasped weakly. ‘You want my chaps to attack policemen?’

‘Got it in one,’ the Colonel replied.

‘But isn’t that against the law?’

‘My dear good man, you are already an accessory to a conspiracy to hijack an island,’ the Colonel reminded him, making his listener’s knees quiver in his neat, flannel trousers. ‘Compared with that bopping the odd bobby hardly merits a “taken into consideration”. Now, here’s what ap Gryfydd wants you to do . . .’

While the Colonel issued his orders, the poor Major stood rigidly at attention at his end of the phone, his free arm at his side and his thumb in line with the seam of his trousers. His only contribution to the conversation was a recurring ‘I see’.

This was less than true. Tears had misted his eyes and were running freely down his apple cheeks. Only a part of his mind was listening to the Colonel but the other, larger part was touring his garden saying goodbye to his greenhouse, to the shrubs, the lawn and the flower beds. Oddly, Madge was not included in the touching farewell. But it is to the Major’s credit that, reluctant though he was, it never occurred to him for an instant to ignore the Colonel’s orders.

On 11 November at the police headquarters in Caernarfon, a building which resembles a pre-World War Two Odeon, the forty-man Tad Task Force assembled to receive its briefing from the superintendent who would lead the assault. Inevitably he was a Scot. There had been yet another successful TV series based on the police and its hero was a tough, no-nonsense Glaswegian with a heart of gold. By 1985 at the HQ of the Metropolitan Police, preoccupation with its public image had become obsessional. Officers above the rank of sergeant attended compulsory personality projection courses at the police TV training college at Hendon. The appointment of Angela Rippon as the first lady Commissioner of the Metropolitan Police was received with universal approbation. Given this mood, the success of the TV series meant that for any tough, no-nonsense Glaswegian the stairway of promotion became an escalator. The heart-of-gold was an optional extra. Superintendent Hector

McDairmaid, who was among the first to leap on the escalator, had a heart of gold so small it wouldn't have filled a medium-sized tooth. As to the rest, he was devoid of nonsense and unquestionably tough. He had, in addition, that gift of self regard, unique to some Scotsmen, which enabled him to invest even the lightest utterance with deep significance. When Superintendent McDairmaid wished you 'Good Morning' he gave the words equal gravity and value to, say, the Gettysburg Address. At the very least he seemed to bestow on the receiver of the greeting his own closely guarded and secret knowledge of the quality of that particular morning. He was, in short, a thundering bore. And he had less attractive qualities. He was the stuff of which prison guards are made: he was a bully. A sandy man with faded freckles that gave his skin the colour and texture of underdone toast, he had the eyes of an insecure anaconda and he was at his happiest when he was addressing, as he was now, a squad of silent underlings.

Swagger stick under his arm, his uniform might have been a second, anxious skin, so nervously did it hug his spare body. The highly-polished brim of his peaked cap heliographed wildly in the harsh electric light of the parade room at the HQ. He jerked, rather than walked, up and down; a nightmare impersonation of Wilson, Kepple and Betty, his regulation boots winking their heliographs back to his cap.

'Now pay attention. Get a hold o'yousel's. You, laddie. Stop waving aboot like piss in the wind!' He pointed his stick at a young constable who had blinked unhappily under his glare.

'The objects of the exercise,' he continued. 'One. Tae return the isle of Tad to the United Kingdom. Two. Tae feel the collars of the island population who have been behaving in a manner calculated to cause a breach of the peace . . .'

'All of them, sir?' A young constable could not help himself. 'There are two thousand of them.'

'Silence!' McDairmaid screamed, transfixing the young policeman with his snake eyes. 'If there's bloody two thousand people transgressing and disturbing the police – I mean the peace—' he corrected the Freudian slip unconvincingly, 'I want their collars felt.'

Apart from McDairmaid only TV scriptwriters used that dated phrase any more. He had, of course, copied it from them. Sensing that only similarity to the hero of the recent TV series had brought him notice and promotion he had made a deep study of his character.

'We en-bus at twenty-two hundred hours. We will be taken by civilian coach tae Penrhyn harbour. From there senior boys from the sea cadets will ferry us across the straits in inflatables.'

'In the dark?' Plainly the young constable was fated to spend his life pushing doors marked 'pull'.

'Of course in the dark, sonny. We don't want them to know we're coming.'

'But won't they hear the inflatables, Superintendent?'

'Aye, but they'll no ken the boats are full of policemen, will they? Let's get on, for God's sake.

'Now then, we will form up on Byndrynkin Pier. There you will be deployed into units of three men. It is not possible to say what sort of opposition we will meet. They're only a bunch of yokels so it will no be much, I shouldn't think. Our first objective is the police station.' He walked across the room to a blackboard on which had been pinned a large scale map. He tapped it with his cane. 'Right?

'Once there we will liaise with the island police. Naturally I shall assume command of both forces. The local chap's obviously not up to it or he would never have let the situation get out of hand in the first place.

'Oh, by the way, I have not seen fit to inform him of our landing. I don't know if he can keep his mouth shut. These swede-bashing bobbies have pretty loose tongues in my experience. So he'll be as surprised as the rest of them, nae doot.

'I think that's all. Now, are there any questions?'

There were none and presently the Task Force filed out to the car-park where two very elderly coaches awaited them. Behind the wheel of the first a curious figure sat. He wore a knitted cap in alternate stripes of red and what may once have been white. The cap had been crammed so far over his head that the hem had become entangled with the rims of his wire-framed spectacles. A beard the colour and texture of a cast-off wire brush took care of the rest of the face. Indeed, it grew in such profusion that it all but covered his oily T-shirt. Behind the spectacles, which gave him the appearance of a demented owl, Mog Pritchard's eyes darted apprehensively. Mog was uneasy in the presence of policemen, even on the rare occasions when he had no reason to be. The sight of forty, not only in one place but advancing upon him, affected him deeply. He hoped they wouldn't notice that the Road Fund licence on his coach was a Guinness label and the one on the rear coach was twelve months out of date.

In the event the Superintendent was too stunned by the overall picture of the two decrepit vehicles to single out individual failings.

'What the hell are they?' It was almost a squeal. The Welsh superintendent who had come out of the building with him permitted himself a brief, guarded smile. The decision to send in a force of Saxon policemen had not been very well received by the local force.

'These are the vehicles the trawler companies use to bring off their crews. The Chief Constable took the view they would attract less attention than a fleet of police cars. You did say you wanted to keep a low profile.'

McDairmaid let his eyes range over the dusty, decrepit buses. The only clean areas were the ones on which children had traced obscenities in the dust. The brown paint on the bodywork was peeling and globules of mud punctuated the legend 'MOG PRITCHARD. COACH PROP'. It wasn't even recent mud.

'Man,' he said, 'yon profile's low enough to put its head in the sand like a bloody ostrich.'

A sudden sense that this was not, after all, to be the easy operation he envisaged gripped him. The Welsh policemen he had met since his arrival were masters of eloquent silence. They might almost have disapproved of the operation, he thought. But that was nonsense, he told himself. Nevertheless he put the next question with some trepidation.

'The Super I'm liaising with on Tad. Good fellow, is he?'

'Oh, one of the best. Grand chap. Reg'lar old-fashioned thief-taker.'

'Thank God for that.'

'Yes, indeed. Mind you, you might not find him quite as helpful as we have been.'

McDairmaid's eyebrows shot for refuge into the brim of his hat.

'No, indeed,' the other man went on. 'Understandable, though. You see he was Sir Huw's RSM in the war.'

It was the final blow. Raising his cane weakly to his cap brim Superintendent McDairmaid made his farewells and with a baleful glare at Mog climbed up the steps into the first bus.

'If it bloody goes, go!' he ordered, only to collapse in an undignified heap on the front seat as, with a lurch, the coach moved off.

Although none of the occupants of either coach was physically sick, the ride from Caernarfon to the harbour was a splendid rehearsal for the sea crossing. When the patrol group stumbled out of the coaches onto the jetty the faint odour of demoralisation hung in the air. The results of travelling at high speed down country lanes in a swaying bus that smelled like the armpit of a trawlerman's jersey were only too apparent.

Their preoccupation prevented them from noticing that Mog had slipped away, oozing across the jetty like an obnoxious fog. Habitually furtive, he sidled into a telephone box, rendering it unfit for human occupation for some days to come. But the message he phoned to his brother-in-law on Tad was gratefully received.

'Forty of the buggers. And me with no Road Tax. Reckon they'll be with you in half an hour.'

Superintendent McDairmaid was not a thoughtful man. Yet even he thought it wise to give his men fifteen minutes to recover from the coach journey before he ordered them to embark. Unfortunately, by the time they had recovered, the inflatables had dropped with a falling tide and they were nine feet below the jetty. Encumbered with riot shields and truncheons, getting aboard was not easy. The policemen had to climb down a stanchion the width of a telegraph pole using iron spikes driven at intervals into its sides. Although only four policemen fell into the water, embarkation was considerably delayed. They had barely reached the centre of the straits when the planes attacked.

CHAPTER NINE

The only indication the Superintendent had of danger came when his flotilla was suddenly illuminated by the headlights of a line of Land Rovers drawn up on Byndrynkin harbour wall. He had just recovered from his surprise when the first flour bomb burst on his head.

The Flying Club had finally decided to use flour bombs after three heated meetings of the committee. Mrs Batty wanted sporting guns lashed to the fuselage below the cockpit. *Blue Max* had been shown on TV for the ninety-eighth time and it always had an unsettling effect on club members. But even Welch was surprised at the degree of blood-thirstiness Mrs Batty evinced. It was a great relief when Meredith Bread Rolls carried the meeting with his suggestion of flour bombs. The Club had enormous fun training. For several days they practised bombing a marked sheet on the airstrip. They were delighted at the spectacle the bags of flour made as they burst.

Superintendent McDairmaid was less enthusiastic when the second flour bag hit him in the chest.

Dazzled by the powerful beams of the headlamps, he had stood in the prow of the inflatable, goggling, as five aircraft, flying in formation, bore down on him. The opening bars of the Dam Busters' March was blaring from the tape recorder which Mrs Batty was playing in her cockpit. Then the bags of flour hit him, coating his immaculate blues with white flour. Unbalanced, he fell backwards over the side, and with a loud cry and a louder splash was lost to sight.

As the planes scored more direct hits other policemen joined him in the water. Some were struck, others leapt to get out of the way of the planes which were flying dangerously low. Soon the water was filled with shouting policemen. When the last policeman hit the water the Sea Cadets, who were in on the plan, put their boats about and headed back for Penrhyn.

On a headland ap Gryfydd danced with joy.

'Got the buggers,' he chortled. Then taking the hand-set of a walkie-talkie from Colonel ap Coch, who stood disapproving at his side, he called up Captain Bill. The harbour pilot was laying offshore in the leading boat of three cutters.

'All yours, skipper,' he reported. From the sea they soon heard the sound of the boats' engines starting.

'I only hope none of the poor devils drown,' ap Coch said severely. 'I do not approve of the deliberate drowning of policemen.'

'Not a chance, Alun. I've got Meurig Raisin Balls and those other devils who poach my salmon downstream with Seine nets. If the blasted salmon can't get past them a great lumbering bobby ought to be child's play. The ones that Captain Bill misses will be netted safe as houses.'

'I'm relieved to hear it.'

Stunned by the attack the demoralised invaders were apprehensive when they were first pulled out of the water. It was a relief when they were greeted with steaming mugs of tea, heavily laced with whisky. They gladly accepted the crews' advice to get out of their wet clothes and to wrap themselves in dry blankets.

They were so relieved at the prospect of dry land that when they stumbled off the cutters onto Byndrynkin Pier none of them noticed that their clothes were not brought ashore with them. It was only when the stern lights of the three boats were flickering back at them over the water that one policeman, perhaps less wet than the rest, shouted: 'My bloody uniform!' Soon all forty, clutching their blankets like shawls, were roaring for the boats. They might have been fishwives wailing the departure of their menfolk. Certainly many were using the sort of language which those ladies are said to have employed. But it was no use. Their shouting died away and the policemen began to examine their surroundings. It was not a sight to warm the heart of anyone clad only in a blanket and government issue boots. The jetty was deserted and the town silent. The Groeslon was officially closed, although in the back kitchen business was brisk as reporters phoned their despatches of the first invasion of Tad since the Vikings. And on the roof photograhers with infra-red flash were getting some remarkable pictures.

Outside not a light showed in any window. Only the keenest eye could have caught the occasional twitch of a lace curtain as one after the other the good folk of Byndrynkin enjoyed the spectacle of the discomfited invaders. They, in contrast, were not enjoying themselves at all. Nights on Tad have a Gothic quality. In the velvet dark monsters are discernible in every shadow. In the village street, gas lamps were the only source of light: a blue-tinged radiance that flickered on the cobbled setts of the main street. And at the end of the street, an apocalyptic figure, stood Chief Superintendent Idris Jones, MM, RSM (rtd).

Superintendent McDairmaid made a less distinguished figure, but he was beyond caring. The reassuring sight of a police uniform called to him as from vasty deeps. With a wild cry he stumbled up the street, an incongruous figure in his blanket. His naked legs were blue with cold and his heavy leather boots squelched as he ran.

Superintendent Jones watched him, unmoved and unmoving. He was still seething at the snub he saw in sending strange policemen into his bailliwick without so much as a by-your-leave. He was quite prepared to make McDairmaid suffer for it.

'Good evening, sir,' he said with dangerous formality as the other came near. 'Is something the matter?'

'Matter? Matter? 'Course there's something the bloody matter.'

Superintendent Jones raised a hand in admonishment. 'Language, sir. Might be children about.'

McDairmaid looked wildly about him at the deserted street.

'Children? What bloody children? Bugger the children. Listen to me. My men have been bombed. Bloody great aeroplanes swooping down on us dropping bombs.'

Superintendent Jones looked suddenly suspicious.

'Not been drinkin', have we?' He sniffed and caught the aroma of whisky with which McDairmaid's tea on the cutter had been generously and deliberately laced.

'I see,' said the Superintendent as he caught its passing. His disapproving glance now seemed to take in for the first time the blanket with which McDairmaid struggled to cover himself. Clearly, the glance said, a participant in orgies, hallucinating as like as not. Staggering down the public highway, indecently dressed and reeking of drink. With a sigh he unfastened his tunic pocket and took out a notebook and pencil.

'I wonder if you would be so good as to give me your name and address?'

The nightmare was gathering the Scotsman to its bosom. Behind him, wrapped in their blankets like disgruntled Sioux, his men were shuffling, disconsolate, up the streets in ones or twos or standing in dispirited huddles on the jetty. McDairmaid knew that they looked to him for leadership. He would be the laughing stock of the Met. for the rest of his career if he did not get control of the situation.

'My name,' he began, 'is Superintendent Hector McDairmaid and my address is Metropolitan Police HQ, London.'

The Welsh Superintendent lifted his pencil in warning. 'Come, come, sir. This is no joke. Impersonating a police officer is a very serious matter.'

'I'm no impersonating, ye damned fool!' McDairmaid was shouting now. 'I *am* a policeman!'

Jones was enjoying himself hugely, if undetectably.

'Now, now, sir. No shouting, if you please. Disturbing the peace. Not very nice. You've clearly had a good time. Don't spoil it. Don't want to have to lock you up.'

'Lock me up? But I am, I really am, a police officer.'

'Then there's no problem, is there?'

'Isn't there?'

'Good heavens, no. All you have to do is show me your warrant card.'

'??????????'

'Your warrant card. You know what a warrant card is?'

Beside himself with rage and humiliation McDairmaid could only stutter.

'Warrant card?' he managed to get out at last. 'I've lost it, haven't I? It was in my uniform.'

'And what happened to your uniform?'

'Well, these sailors told us to get undressed. Then they must have taken our clothes away.'

'Sailors, eh? Told you to get undressed, eh? Oh, I see.'

Superintendent Jones's voice missed not a nuance. When McDairmaid realised the ambiguity of what he had said the skin that had been blue with cold became rosy with embarrassment.

'You don't see at all, you dirty minded sod. I mean they took them off to dry after they fished us out of the water.'

'The water? Oh, you've had a boating accident? Why didn't you say so . . .'

'Accident?' McDairmaid was on the verge of tears. 'It was no bloody accident, you swede-bashing oaf. I've told you. We were dive-bombed. These planes dropped bags of flour on us. Dammit, we were on our way to help you.'

'Help me?' The Superintendent was withering in his scorn. 'Dressed up like a lot of drowning Red Indians? What were you going to do? Teach me how to make smoke signals?'

'We were going to help you quell the revolution.'

'Revolution?' Superintendent Jones looked about him at the silent town. 'What revolution? The only disturbance I've had tonight is from you and that bunch of refugees from the Maid of the Mountains.'

'Now lookee here,' began McDairmaid.

'No!' broke in the Superintendent. 'You look here. You come poncing up the street half naked and stinking of drink and you tell me you've been undressed by a bunch of sailors. Then you give me some cock and bull story about being a police officer and being dive-bombed while you were on your way to help me quell a revolution.

'Do you realise how many offences you have committed in the last half hour?' He ticked them off on his fingers. 'Disturbing the peace, drunk and disorderly, indecent exposure, impersonating a police officer, for starters. If I took you into custody now, my lad, there'd be steeple chasing on Mars by the time you got out of the nick.'

It must have been the 'my lad' that broke McDairmaid. With a howl of rage he raised both hands in the air, fists clenched. Unfortunately, in doing so, he released his grip on his blanket which fell to the ground revealing him unappetising in his nudity. McDairmaid was beyond caring. He was literally dancing with rage.

'Ye Welsh git,' he roared. 'Ye stupid lummix! See they?' and he pointed behind him with a jerk of the thumb at his bedraggled followers. 'Special Patrol Group. Highly skilled. Every one a judo expert. Threaten me, would ye, ye bliddy wooden top? One word from me and they'd spring at your throat. I could get youse torn tae bits.'

'Yes,' Jones told him, purring with satisfaction. 'And that little speech could get you about three years, my Haggis chewing friend.'

As McDairmaid watched, the Superintendent took out a whistle and blew it. The nightmare finally took over. From every dark doorway stepped a soldier carrying a rifle.

'Major Tufton-Bellis!' Jones shouted, and an unhappy voice answered, 'Yes.' 'I am arresting these men in blankets on a number of charges pertaining to breaches of the peace. I call upon your soldiers to aid me. I want you to march them to the Parish Institute where they are to be locked up and placed under guard.'

He turned to McDairmaid. 'You will be kept there in custody until the next session of the magistrates' court.'

McDairmaid knew when he was beaten. 'When is that, for God's sake,' he begged.

'A week on Tuesday,' he was told.

'And who's the magistrate?'

'Why,' Jones told him, 'Sir Huw ap Gryfydd. Who else? You see how much better it would have been all round, had you been a police officer, if you'd warned the local force of your intended arrival?'

And suddenly McDairmaid did see. In a blinding flash he saw everything. He was still shaking his head in sorrow as he was marched into captivity with his men.

ap Gryfydd was waiting in the kitchen of the Groeslon. When he saw Jones come in he pushed his way through the crowd of reporters to whom he had been giving a post-invasion interview. The two men retired to the fire where ap Gryfydd listened with satisfaction to the superintendent's report.

'Well done, Sarn't Major,' he said at last. 'Everyone safe, I trust? Good. No casualties?'

'Only the Scotchman's ego,' the superintendent told him. 'But we can't leave them in the Institute indefinitely. It's the whist drive on Thursday.'

'We'll have a word with them in the morning. In the meantime I've had Will Looms take them over a few cases of beer and there'll be sandwiches in half an hour. Hate them to think there was anything personal.'

ap Gryfydd was all benevolence. The events of the evening had taken twenty years off him. The superintendent was less happy.

'Tonight was grand,' he admitted, 'but we'll not get away with it twice. Fortunately that Scotchman's a fool and with a bit of goading he gave me very good reason to arrest him. Insisted on conducting his own prosecution, you might say. In any case, Colwyn Bay will be sufficiently embarrassed at letting strangers into my bailliwick without telling me. They won't want to make too much fuss. But as soon as I see the Met. men's warrant cards I'll have to let them go. Where are their uniforms, by the way?'

'That's the trouble,' ap Gryfydd grinned wickedly. 'Captain Bill's landed them on Becod. Must have forgotten them when he was putting the policemen ashore. Naturally I've ordered them to be dried. But Mrs Rose tells me they will take all night. With the tides it will be noon at the earliest before I can get them back to you.'

'There's a pity,' said the superintendent.

'Yes indeed,' ap Gryfydd replied. He looked for a moment at the queue of reporters waiting for the hotel's only public phone. 'Be all over the papers by then, shouldn't wonder. *Duw!*'

The next morning it *was* all over the papers and it was all over the face of the Secretary of State for Wales as he burst into the Field Marshal's office waving a copy of the

Daily Express–Mail. He had chosen his paper carefully with a view to brandishing it about. *The Times*, he felt, was too restrained: the *Sun* too vulgar with its picture of the naked McDairmaid, blanket round his ankles and looking back over his shoulder. The caption read simply 'Policeman's Lot'.

'Have you seen it?' he demanded. 'It's a bloody mockery. We'd have done better to send in the Sea Cadets and let the Met. provide the boat crews.'

The Field Marshal had seen the *Express–Mail*. He had also seen the *Star*, the *Daily Mirror*, the *Sun*, the *Daily Telegraph* and *The Times*. With each deeply satisfying read his glee had increased. But he presented the Secretary of State with a grave face.

'Bad show,' he said sympathetically. 'But I did minute you about the desirability of putting in troops. Tricky things seaborne landings. Need highly trained chaps.'

The Secretary of State was uncomfortably aware that the minute existed and would be seen by the PM. But it had been unnecessarily malicious of the Field Marshal to rub it in. Nothing else would have induced the Secretary of State to break his promise to Shovel's ADC.

'The ones in the cupboard, I suppose?' he said nastily, and had the satisfaction of seeing the Field Marshal blush. 'Obviously a leak somewhere,' he went on. 'Or how did they have time to lay on their defences?'

'Local, I should think,' the Field Marshal replied hurriedly, and changed the subject. 'I suppose it will now be your wish for me to send in my chaps? I rather thought Marine Commandos?'

'Field Marshal. Once and for all. No troops. Good God, man. You know the Russians have offered to send in technical advisers and there have been messages of solidarity from Cuba, East Germany, Hungary, Poland, Czechoslovakia and the South Wales steelworkers? I tell you it's dashed serious. If we send in soldiers now we could well start World War Three. The PM's furious. This morning's poll shows that fifty-six per cent of our people are in favour of granting Tad independence and another fourteen per cent want Home

Rule for Cornwall. I tell you, unless something is done, and done quickly, we will be lucky to be governing Surrey by the end of the week.'

'What do you propose?'

'I'm sending my Permanent Secretary, Sir Pelham Effyngham-Blynd, to Tad.'

'Effyngham-Blynd! Good Lord! Are you sure that's wise?'

'D'ye know him?'

'We were at Eton. Called him "Plum" then. Very apt. Small and round. When he got bigger and even rounder it was changed to "Victoria". But he was such a damned old woman they were calling him Queen Victoria in the sixth. At least, I think that's why.'

The Secretary smiled, a wintry smile.

'Pompous devil, I grant you. But able. Always does well on motorway inquiries. I thought of him for this because he did such a grand job on the Isle of Man. He practically arranged Manx independence single-handed. Won the most favourable kipper tariff, too. Thoroughly deserved his "K". The PM's devoted to kippers.'

The Field Marshal thought it wiser to talk of other matters. It never did to criticise the Secretary of State's choice in anything; but he had grave doubts about 'Queen' Victoria. Impressive enough to look at, but not much in the way of guts, as he remembered. Sir Pelham Effyngham-Blynd was a large man: in everything, that is, except vision. In that he was minuscule. But an eye-glass on a black ribbon and a gold watch chain shared his waistcoat front and there was ample room for both, for Sir Pelham was a man of generous proportions. Although his heavily-jowled pink face had the texture and consistency of nursery junket he was stately and commanding. When he bore down on you it was like being run down by a ship of the line. So vivid was the impression that one expected his waistcoat pockets to open and reveal banks of cannon. Alas, Sir Pelham's heaviest armament was the quibble, delivered in a high-pitched, supercilious whine. With his embossed briefcase and soft kid shoes and his Mandarin air, the Field Marshal thought, he might have been assembled expressly to infuriate Sir Huw ap

Gryfydd. Nothing would have induced the Field Marshal to wish to be anything as anonymous as a fly on the wall, but he would have given much to be present at the first meeting of the two men.

CHAPTER TEN

'That you, Meredith? Gareth Jenkyn here. Seen the papers?'

The Chairman of the Red Hand of Glyndwr Society had indeed seen the papers and his hand on the phone shook with patriotic fervour.

'*Arglwydd*, yes,' he said. 'That showed the bloody *Sais*. Battle of Pilleth all over again. Remember when Owain's Children swept down the hill and massacred the Earl of March's army in the Valley of the Lugg . . .'

But Gareth was in no mood for past battles; he had a war of his own to win. In any case his knowledge of Welsh medieval history was sketchy.

'Yes indeed, Chairman. But we must concentrate on our own battle. Don't you think we ought to start nudging about the Court of Human Rights? In all the excitement it does seem to have been overlooked. The news is good, yes. But we've only won the first skirmish. We have still to win the war.'

Gareth had convinced himself that the whole idea of independence had come from him. ap Gryfydd and the Gorsedd were really his puppets. A potential Napoleon he was now ready for the next stage in his Grand Design.

'What news from the Blair woman?'

'Saw her yesterday, as a matter of fact. She seems to think ap Gryfydd's gone cold on the idea for some reason.'

'Christ, we can't have that. Full independence. The People will accept nothing less. We've got to wipe out that Referendum fiasco.'

'But, Gareth, surely that was the People? After all, it was four to one against.'

'Manipulation by the media, Mr Chairman. That never represented the *true* view. No. Today Tad, TOMORROW WALES. That was the resolution of the committee. Carried unanimous.'

'I don't quite see how we're going to do it. Manipulation

always seems that hard when we try to do it ourselves. Funny, really. Other people are doin' it all the time, according to you.'

'A leak, Mr Chairman.'

'A leek?'

'L–E–A–K. Leak.'

'But how?'

'Easy. Them reporters still drinkin' their heads off in the Groeslon?'

'Oh, yes.'

'Capitalist lackeys. Tell you what, we'll go down lunchtime and just drop a few hints, like. Get a free drink out of it. Fair play. We can tell them about the parchment and put them onto the Blair woman. She'll spill everything and once it's in the papers ap Gryfydd'll have to go ahead with it. Fait-a-bloody-compli, boy.'

'But it's a breach of confidence, Gareth. Told me in confidence she did.'

Gareth sighed. Sometimes he wondered if the People were worth saving.

'Larger issues, Mr Chairman. We've all got to make compromises of conscience for the greater good.'

'I suppose so . . .' Meredith began.

'Groeslon, twelve sharp, then,' said Gareth, and rang off before his Chairman could object.

He was right about the reporters. Ashton and the others rose to the fly like trout in May. They needed another story badly to stave off their recall to their offices in Manchester. They'd been able to stretch out this job handsomely and the expenses were so good that some would actually make more than they spent. Another three weeks of this and even Ashton, who believed in travelling through life First Class, would show a profit on his expense sheet. It had been a good innings. They had spun the declaration of independence out for several weeks with all the follow-ups and features they had found. Then, just as they were running out of ideas, had come the invasion; and following that the court case at which ap Gryfydd had fined all the policemen forty shillings – the island had quickly abandoned the metric system thus providing yet another series of follow-ups. The 2p. coin was tuppence again, the 10p. a florin and 50 pence was a ten shilling piece now. The values were not altered but everyone thought the names much more homely. Next there had been the story of the repatriation of the policemen, all their uniforms smartly pressed by the maids of Plas Becod and each given a packet of sandwiches for the journey.

The offer of help from behind the Iron Curtain had been a godsend on a slow day. 'Russians for Tad?' struck just the right note of unease. But the days that followed had been quiet. How long they could spin out the job now depended on news desk nerve. All the desks were waiting for the first news editor to make the decision that the story was dead. When the first pulled his men out the others would follow. The story would be handed over to the local correspondent who would make a small fortune writing 'holding stories' and the 'pack' would be dispersed until they met again on another story. The suggestion that Tad was going to fight for its independence in the international courts gave the story a new dimension.

As Ashton said: 'Takes it right out of the *Passport to Pimlico* class.'

Miss Blair was at once nervous and flattered when a group of newspapermen and TV crews arrived at her cottage door. As, one by one, they practised their insidious charm, admiring her garden and praising her scholarship, her 'no comments' became less convincing. Finally she agreed there were grounds for believing Tad was an independent kingdom. The response to this item of news was so flattering, the interest so gratifying, that it was not long before she had told them almost the whole story. She told no one about the parchment, though.

Sir Pelham Effyngham-Blynd heard the news when he was handed into his first class compartment by his aide Tim Crisp and unfolded the morning paper to pass time on his journey to Wales.

ap Gryfydd's comments were guarded but he had confirmed the truth of the story and that had been enough for the reporters. Miss Blair had been quoted in full. Pshaw, thought the Mandarin. He'd come across several biddies like her in his career and ridden them into the ground.

'Frightful business, Sir Pelham.' Crisp broke into his thoughts. 'The Court of Human Rights, I mean.'

'Paper tiger, my boy,' Sir Pelham told him loftily.

'But what if the court goes against us?'

'What of it?'

'It is the judicial arm of the Council of Europe, surely?'

'Fiddlesticks! There exists no obligation on Britain even as a member state to accept the court's jurisdiction. I'm not even sure a private individual has the right to sue.'

'Lawless versus Ireland in 1961?' Crisp, an ambitious lad, had spent the early part of the day mugging up the subject after he had seen the first headline. So had Sir Pelham. He had also seen a paper long before he had been handed *The Times* on the train. In fact, the *Sun* was delivered to his house every morning. He pretended it was for his housekeeper.

'A dubious precedent. Quite true the judgment in that case upheld the right of individual petitioners, but I doubt if the precedent is sound.'

'But surely, Sir Pelham, Tad would petition as a state rather than ap Gryfydd as an individual.'

'Not with conviction. Believe me, there isn't even legislative machinery to bind a member state to international law. Think of the Isle of Man birching.'

Sir Pelham had. Often and with pleasure. Occasional light flagellation in a Very Respectable House was the only sexual indulgence he had permitted himself since the Vassal tribunal.

'Or that business of the use of the tawse in Scottish schools. So far as I am aware our Scots friends are still tawsing away.'

The thought obviously pleased him.

'No, no, my boy,' he added merrily, 'I think we can safely ignore the Supreme Court in Strasbourg. The judicial arm of the Council of Europe has evidently not the strength of that which wields the birch.'

Discussing such subjects with a handsome young man awakened more than one appetite. Smiling owlishly he took out his hunter and consulted it.

'It lacks but a minute to 12.30,' he announced. 'Shall we go along and see if they are ready for us in the restaurant car?'

He rose majestically and made for the corridor. Following in his wake Crisp asked: 'Is that the view of the Secretary of State, sir?'

Sir Pelham paused in the doorway of the compartment, filling it with ease. He raked Crisp with a withering glance.

'*I am* the view of the Secretary of State,' he announced grandly, and swept out.

Tim Crisp shook his head sadly and followed him. He was a decent young man, handsome with golden hair and a trim, lean body. There was about him an air of imminent tennis. The story of the little island fighting for its freedom had found an echo in his soul. He came from a long line of Backs-to-the-wall Crisps. There had been a Crisp in the Battle of Britain, at Mons, on the North-West Frontier and at Waterloo. Their favourite odds, as a family, had always been ten to one. Though he was sufficiently Civil Service to hide it, he had felt a distinct tremor of sympathy when he had been briefed for Tad.

Sir Pelham had wondered why ap Gryfydd's comments had been uncharacteristically guarded in the newspaper. The answer was five feet six inches high, pretty as paint, vivid as lightning, with the look of a wanton gypsy and answered to the name of Ceri. None of the ap Gryfydds belonged to the age in which they were born. Ceri, Sir Huw's daughter, was pure Restoration. She might have been created by Lely. She also had a fiery temper and it had exploded when she read in her office of a London publisher about the capture of forty policemen. Pausing only to demand and get indefinite leave from her managing director who was terrified of her she had leapt into her lethal sports car and headed north.

Gunner Atkinson, who brought her across the strait in the punt, could see she was seething with anger. Wisely he did not attempt a word after his initial greeting.

'Is my father home?' she had demanded. When Atkinson told her he was she had merely said: 'Good.' Not another word passed between them until the punt was landed. Then, leaping ashore and leaving Atkinson with her bags, she said,

‘Thank you’ as she stumped up the foreshore.

A tiger, thought Atkinson fondly. But a good mannered one, fair play.

ap Gryfydd’s growl of delight when she burst into the library where he was trying in vain to stay awake after lunch quickly trailed away.

‘Father! I suppose you realise you’ll be in prison by the end of the month.’

The growl became fretful. If it had been anyone else it might have sounded apprehensive. The trouble was that ap Gryfydd was becoming bored with UDI. He had climbed into the saddle of a hobby horse and found himself riding a runaway stallion. He’d loved the invasion but now it was all administration and he hated it. That very evening he was meeting ap Coch’s confounded ‘Government of All the Talents’. Damn silly name for a lot of old fogeys. Bound to pester him to do things. More damn bumpf. And then there was that business of the Court of Human Rights. Blast that woman’s eyes. Why hadn’t she told him he would have to attend in person? Go abroad, indeed. Abroad was dreadful. ap Gryfydds only went abroad to kill foreigners. Absolutely no point in going otherwise. Filthy beasts. You’d only got to see their public lavatories. No idea about hygiene.

‘How is it,’ he demanded of Ceri, ‘that the blasted French have produced all those clever painters and play writers and people. Yet they don’t seem to be able to train a single plumber?’

But Ceri had undergone a lifetime’s experience of her father’s tangential conversation. She just ignored the digression.

‘What on earth are you up to?’ she demanded. ‘I’m the laughing stock of my office. My MD actually proposed we should get someone to write a novel about you.’

ap Gryfydd’s eyes lit up. He had an endearing vanity.

‘And a good idea, too. Better than those dirty books you’re bringing out now.’

Ceri’s firm had brought out a coffee table book of highly praised erotica which had succeeded the adventures of rabbits and badgers as required reading. She was proud of the book which had won the Women's Institute Literary Prize, but refused to be put off.

'I said, what are you up to?'

'Up to? Up to? No way to talk to your father, *cariad.*' He was all innocence now.

'And don't call me *cariad*. I'm certainly no sweetheart of yours today. And I hope you won't expect me to visit you in Walton.'

'Don't be silly, girl. No one's going to Walton, Ceri *fach.*'

'And I'm not your little Ceri either.'

'*Duw!*' said her father, his huge eyes swimming. 'D'you know you're the very image of your mother. Got her wicked tongue, too.'

'And you can just stop your crying act. I'm not going to be soft-soaped this time.'

But, of course, she was. Poor old thing, she thought, he must be dreadfully lonely. And good-hearted girl that she was the anger she had been feeding for three hundred miles drained away.

'Oh, I give in,' she said, perching on the arm of her father's chair and kissing the top of his head. 'But I can't think what ap Coch was doing letting you get mixed up in this.'

'Letting me, girl? It was his idea,' lied her father brazenly.

CHAPTER ELEVEN

When her father left for his meeting with the 'Government of All the Talents', Ceri watched from the terrace of the Plas until Atkinson had landed him safely on Tad. Then, when they had waved to each other, he started his Land Rover and she returned to the Great Hall where she curled up in a wing chair before a roaring fire. Outside, the December afternoon was swathed in sea mist. Beyond the pool of light from the fire shadows were lengthening. It was the perfect setting through which to run trains of thought and Ceri had one of Flying Scot proportions gathering steam in her mind.

Two reasons had prompted her to leave Plas Becod, which she loved fiercely, for an unsatisfactory life in a glorified bed-sitter and the guerilla warfare of the London publishing world in which she was an executive. Firstly, she wanted a career and she had been determined to make one of her own, outside the sphere of her family's influence. An only child, she felt it was her duty, when her mother died, to return home, but it had not worked. She quickly found that devotion to her father kept peeping out from under the cloak of disapproval her mother had warned her she must always wear to keep him under control. ap Gryfydd, on the other hand, who had no subtlety in love or hate, adored her as he had her mother, openly and unashamedly.

She thought about the curious mixture that was her father. He was a generous landlord to his tenant farmers; a kindly employer to his servants and to the workers on his estate. His farms and cottages were among the first in rural Wales to have electricity, mains drainage and piped water. That was the attractive face of his feudalism, she reflected, as the flames in the fireplace dervish-danced on the log ends. Quietly Grout came in with fresh logs and just as quietly withdrew. Normally he would have chattered as he stacked the logs but today he worked silently. There's something to be said for Celtic sensitivity, she thought. Servants grew old in her father's service. Some of them, she admitted wrily, while still in their early twenties.

The problem was that strangers never understood her father in the way that these, his own people, did. Strangers saw only the other face, the face of the elemental which reinforced the belief that cannibalism was still alive and well and living in rural Wales. It was that face he was showing to the world now as he stood at bay trying to keep his little island world intact. But he was doomed. He was an anachronism. He lived simply, not because he was mean, but because he preferred life that way. His own herds provided him with meat, milk and wool; the Home Farm gave him vegetables for his table and cereals for his bread and beer. Even the wine he drank was fermented in the kitchens of the Plas from island fruits, and, more recently, the cans of grape juice which the trendy Mrs Rose had discovered on her weekly shopping trip to Caernarfon. ap Gryfydd loved the notion that everything he ate and drank had been grown on The Place. It was that philosophy he was defending. And not only for himself but for the rest of the islanders, too. There was no poverty on the island. Even the smallest cottage had land on which to keep a pig and the house cow, to grow vegetables and venerable orchards. She thought of the skyscraper council flats in London. No one in those lived as well as the poorest islanders. The island's schools had excellent teachers, many of them highly qualified men and women who had fled from the mainland to escape from the horrors of urban life. The cottage hospital was a model of its kind and so far her father had resisted efforts to close it and transfer its patients to the overcrowded infirmary on the mainland. But Ceri knew that it was a losing battle. Her father was no match for the bureaucratic juggernaut. He needed an ally, Ceri decided. She wished that her mother were still alive. She had been the perfect partner. Darkly Celtic, her mind had been subtle and devious. She would not have approved of the way ap Gryfydd was handling the enemies. But having expressed disapproval she would have remained at his side, counselling and checking his wilder flights.

And then the answer arrived. The reason that she had

really come home. She was, after all, her mother's daughter. She looked up at the portrait of her over the fireplace. They even looked alike. Why shouldn't I take her place, she thought? She had, after all, survived the purges and politicking of the publishing trade. After those a battle with the Civil Service should be child's play.

She looked again at the portrait over the fireplace. Was it a trick of light and shadow, or was her mother really smiling her approval?

As though on cue the door bell clanged, and after a decent interval Grout materialised at the side of her chair.

'A Mr Crisp, Miss Ceri. From the Government. Come to see ap Gryfydd.'

Ceri smiled up at the portrait. A sign, surely? If that's the way you want it, she thought. To Grout she said, 'Show him in. And you'd better bring the drinks tray.'

Neither Tim Crisp, who had come unwillingly on Sir Pelham's orders to arrange a meeting with Sir Huw, nor Ceri, who was preparing to do battle with a dry stick of a civil servant, was prepared for what each of them saw.

Ceri managed, with the instinctive skill of womankind, to hide her approval of the lean, handsome young man in soft tweeds who was presently shown in. Tim Crisp, who, after all, was a mere man, was less successful in disguising his admiration for the strikingly beautiful girl he saw, curled up like an adorable kitten, in the wing chair.

'Good evening,' said Ceri, coolly. 'I'm afraid my father is at a meeting. Is there anything I can do for you?'

'Good evening,' said the civil servant when he was able to control his admiration. 'I'm Crisp, PA to Sir Pelham Effyngham-Blynd. Actually I was rather hoping to meet your father.'

It was plain that he approved wholeheartedly of the substitute the home team had played.

'Effyngham-Blynd? What a very curious name.'

'I suppose it is really.'

'Sounds somehow rather coarse.'

'Oh, I assure you he isn't. Quite the opposite, in fact.'

'I meant the name. I'm sorry, do go on.'

If a parallel of this conversation were sought, dappling for trout with mayfly would suit admirably. And Crisp, poor fish, was rising to every fly.

'Er . . . he was hoping that your father might kindly consent to see him.'

It wasn't the way Sir Pelham had put it, he thought, with a spasm of guilt. The interview wasn't at all going the way he had planned, but he plunged on, softening the terms of his errand.

'He was rather hoping we might clear up this misunderstanding . . .'

'Misunderstanding?'

The mayfly were deep frozen now.

'Yes, rather. I'm sure it's nothing more than media misrepresentation. This UDI nonsense, I mean.' He laughed, or rather snickered nervously.

'Nonsense?' There was no mistaking the ice in the tone now. 'I can assure you my father doesn't think it at all nonsense. Quite other.'

'But, really, Miss ap Gryfydd . . .'

'Working in your country I've had to anglicise my name to Griffiths.'

'Oh yes? Very nice.'

'Nice? Nice? I don't think it nice at all. I think it quite shameful, in fact.'

'Hardly shameful, surely?'

'No? Tell me, if you came to work in Wales, should you like to change your name?'

'Crisp?' he attempted a rally. 'Bit difficult to Welshify Crisp I should have thought.'

'On the contrary. The Welsh form of Crisp is Crych.'

'Crych?'

'You don't like it?'

'Not much.'

'I'm not exactly in love with Griffiths.'

Poor Tim could not have laid his hand on his heart and said the same. And the feeling was growing, as it often does, with every rebuff. The less friendly Ceri became, the further into his heart went her hook. It was playing havoc with his social manner. And every time he uttered it got worse.

'What's in a name, after all?' he tried with a grin that was strained and foolish.

'Why must you English always hide behind Shakespeare?'

'I beg your pardon?'

'It's true. Whenever you are at a loss you trundle out some clumsy platitude by Shakespeare. Celts don't do it. You don't hear us quoting Dafydd ap Gwillym by the yard.'

'Shakespeare doesn't write clumsy platitudes, Miss Griff . . . ,' he began, piqued. 'Dafydd ap who?'

'Gwillym.'

'A local man? I don't believe I've met him.'

'Hardly surprising. He's been dead about six hundred years. He happens to be our national poet. And considered by most scholars to be one of the finest European lyric poets.'

'Oh, I see. A Welsh Shakespeare,' said Tim brightly, intending no umbrage.

'You plainly don't see at all,' replied Ceri, taking it. 'He was nothing of the kind. He at least was original. He didn't go around stealing other people's plots and getting involved in dubious property deals.'

'Oh, I say! That's a bit thick, surely? Your chap wrote plays, then?'

'My chap, as you are pleased to call him, wrote poetry. Some of the finest poetry of all time, in fact.'

This seemed a much more promising line and Tim plunged after it, unhesitatingly.

'Like Keats?'

'Not at all like Keats. Keats used to put red pepper on his tongue so that his claret would taste cooler. I can't imagine Dafydd doing anything so vulgar.'

Tim, who like most young men of his class considered himself, quite wrongly, an amateur of wine, was shocked.

'Are you sure? What a terrible thing to do.'

'I'm glad you agree.'

'Oh, certainly. Absolutely frightful.'

'So's what you are doing to my father.'

Tim was wholly bemused by now. No sooner did he find a

promising opening through which to poke his head than he got it severely drubbed.

'I'm not doing anything to your father,' he protested.

'Well, perhaps not you personally,' she conceded with reluctance. 'That dreadful government of yours.'

'It's your government, too.'

'Isn't that rather the point at issue?'

He decided to throw in the towel.

'Oh, Miss Griffiths, can't we begin again? I really don't want to fight you.'

Unconsciously he had played a master stroke. He looked so vulnerable, so like a puppy that has been beaten with a slipper that her heart went out to him. She found puppies irresistible.

In fact there were two conversations going on between them. The one with the mouth was defensive and brittle. But there was a second conversation, a quite different one, going on in the eyes of these two young people and at last Tim picked up a word or two of that one and became bolder.

'I do wish you wouldn't treat me like an enemy,' he said. 'No, please don't interrupt. In a way I admire the stand your father is taking. But I do wish you could make him see that his case is hopeless. It is, you know. He can't hope to beat HMG. Don't you see they've had hundreds of years' experience of being nasty. Beating off the Special Patrol Group was marvellous. Great fun. And if it's any satisfaction, he's made an international laughing stock of some very senior people. But this is 1985. This isn't a *Whisky Galore* world any more. And they're not still issuing *Passports to Pimlico*. They're just old films on Christmas TV. The real world isn't at all like that. Governments are only assemblies of people, you know. And people hate being made figures of fun. Especially the sort of pompous people who run governments, and they've got some very nasty methods of fighting back.'

'I suppose you approve of that,' Ceri broke in.

'Oh, don't be so stupid.'

'I beg your pardon?'

'I mean it. Do you honestly think I'd be talking to you like this if I approved of what Queen Victoria will do to gain an advantage?'

'Queen Victoria?'

'My boss, Sir Pelham. It's his nickname in the department. Oh, yes, we're quite human under our red tape wrappings. Believe me, he knows more ways of being unpleasant than anyone in the Service.'

'You make him sound a monster.'

'Good. Because that is just what he is. Oh, he doesn't look it. No doubt you'll think he's an old maid, but you'll be wrong. Do believe me. You don't get to be a PS in a highly competitive organisation like the Civil Service unless you are very tough indeed. And Sir Pelham's soft centre is on the outside. Inside the marshmallow he's pure tungsten.'

At this moment Grout came in with the drinks tray on which bottles were rattling hospitably. Ceri was glad of the interruption. She had set out deliberately to goad this young man. But her heart had not really been in it; it was more coquetry than dislike. And the things Crisp had just told her so mirrored her own doubts that she felt the clutch of fear. Without the slightest regret she decided to abandon her impregnable tactical position and to accept the shoulder that Tim was so enthusiastically proferring.

When he had accepted a drink she made the first tentative steps towards a peace treaty.

'As a matter of fact,' she admitted, 'I'd already worked that out by myself. But, frankly, I just don't know what to do.'

Tim became at once masterful.

'Good,' he said briskly. 'All you've got to do is to persuade your father to come to a compromise.'

'Persuade? You've not met my father. And I've got a nasty feeling that your Sir Pelham is about the worst negotiator the government could have sent.'

'It sounds as though they are going to be both red rag and bull to each other. Obviously they must not meet.' They were conspirators now and Tim revelled in the knowledge.

'I'll tell him Sir Huw was out. If there is some way you can keep your father busy for a couple of days I'm sure Sir Pelham would be glad of any excuse to return to London.

We're staying at the Groeslon and it's something quite outside his experience. But he mustn't feel he is being snubbed. That would be fatal. Your father will have to be genuinely busy so that he can return to London without losing face. Something he's got rather a lot of,' he added with reckless disloyalty. 'We need something your father is involved in which will make Sir Pelham glad to flee the island. A flood or something. He can't bear discomfort.'

'Herrings in his bed?' offered Ceri helpfully. 'I could arrange it quite easily. One of the fishermen is a great friend of mine.'

Tim found he did not like the sound of the friendship at all.

'No, no. Too clumsy. I suppose you don't know a Celtic witch who could arrange something nasty? An open air orgy? Something of that sort?'

With a cry of joy Ceri launched herself from the armchair, and to his surprise and delight, Tim found himself being hugged. Very briefly, it is true, for Ceri soon recovered herself and retired in confusion to her chair.

'I'm sorry,' she said. 'It was something you said. About orgies.'

'Why? Are we having one? I rather thought they lasted longer.'

'No, silly.'

Always a good sign, thought Tim, when they call you that. He had been considerably heartened by the embrace.

'Tomorrow's December 6, St Friad's Day. Tomorrow night is Friad's *Cwcwll Gêm*.'

'Good God! What's that?'

'It's a pagan rite to placate the spirit of winter. In the old days they used to have a feast to eat up all the perishable food they couldn't preserve through the winter. But the Christians pinched all the old pagan celebrations and turned them into Christian celebrations. You know Christmas isn't really Christmas? It's the feast of Mithras and Easter was originally a rite to welcome spring.'

Tim, who didn't, nodded wisely.

'Well, St Friad wasn't really a saint. She was a Celtic princess. Apparently her father, an Irish king, had arranged one of those political marriages for her, to a rather unpleasant suitor. Well, anyway, on the night before her wedding she gave all her maidens cloaks to make them invisible, then she cut thirteen turfs from a magic meadow and they sailed across the Irish Sea on them to Anglesey. She was a very powerful witch.'

'Good God,' thought Tim, 'she believes it!' And, he thought romantically, how like a Celtic princess she looked herself with the firelight playing on her raven hair.

'They say she turned the Mayor of Cork into a horse, so crossing the Irish Sea on a turf would have been child's play.'

'You sound as though you believe this,' said Tim wonderingly. He'd never met anyone quite like Ceri in his life.

'Of course I don't,' said Ceri unconvincingly. 'I'm just telling you the legend. Apparently she had this hermitage on Anglesey where she worked these spells. And, of course, people began talking about them, her fame spread and it wasn't long before it got back to her father. And he sent warriors to bring her back to Ireland. So once again she had to flee. And that is how she came to Tad.'

'On a turf, I suppose.' Tim was one of those Saxons who are made uneasy by myth.

'How could she?' Ceri replied scornfully. 'The turfs came from the magic meadow. And that was in Ireland.'

'I see, of course. Silly of me. Do go on.'

'She cut rushes, threw them into the sea and they changed into sea trout. She rode to Tad on their backs.'

'With all her maidens?'

'Don't mock. Young sea trout on Tad – we call them Sewyn – have a distinct taste of hay.'

'Sir Pelham won't like that.'

'He'll like what's coming. Just as Friad was stepping ashore her hood – that's what *Cwcwll* means – was blown away. There were some fishermen on the shore when she landed. And when they saw how beautiful she was they ran to retrieve it.

'Unfortunately the wind blew the hood inland and some farm workers began chasing it too. It all ended in the most dreadful battle on the shore and, of course, the hood was ripped to shreds. They all grabbed a piece and took it back to her. You'd have thought she would have been furious, I know I should. But she was very saintly, of course. She said she was touched by their welcome and that she was sure they would fight just as nobly for her if her father's warriors came to kidnap her. And she asked them to re-stage the fight every year on the same day so that everyone would know just what brave fighters the men of Tad were.'

'And do they?'

'Oh, yes. Every year a team of young farmers who drink at the Groeslon – that's the farmers' pub – meet a team of fishermen from the Mermaid – that's the fishermen's pub on the shore. The meeting place is called Traeth Coch. That means the Red Shore and when you've seen the *Cwcwll* you'll know why. There's even an echo of human sacrifice. There's a man in the village who always takes the role of the Fool. And before the game they set fire to his hat. While he's still wearing it. I suppose they used to burn victims at the stake.'

'Is it a rough game?'

'Pretty. The teams stand in a group and the *Cwcwll* is thrown into the middle. The object of the game is to fell as many of the opposing team as you can and get the *Cwcwll* into your own pub. The victors get free beer all night.'

'Sort of terminal rugby football?'

'Got it in one. And the point is that all the pubs on the island have extensions until one a.m.'

'Sir Pelham won't like that. Not one little bit. Rowdy drunks give him a rash.'

'Then he won't like the day after either. Or, come to that, tomorrow afternoon.'

'Oh?'

'No. As you can imagine, the *gêm* – that's game to you *Sais* – is not the sort of thing you go into sober. Especially since most of the players have friends and relatives on the other side. So a warm up starts at around one p.m. and goes on until the game is played.'

'But surely the day after will be pretty quiet? Or don't people get hangovers on Tad?'

'They get them. But they don't admit to them. It's a macho

thing. And, besides, there's Friad's *Gwledd*. That means feast. It's another tradition. Every pub on the island cooks a cauldron of pig's head broth and serves it with jacket potatoes. All free.'

Tim shuddered. 'They needn't fight at all to get rid of Sir Pelham. I'll only have to tell him there's pig's head for lunch and he'll be off to London on the first train.'

They both laughed, but Ceri was soon glum again.

'But what good will it do? We chase out your boss but the problem stays.'

'At least you will have a breathing space and a chance to persuade your father.'

'But what can I say? I've never known him change his mind about anything.'

'He needn't change it now. After all, he's got what he wanted. The GPO won't dare drop the name of the island from letters now. I should think there might even be a chance of the old county status being restored. That's all he ever wanted.'

'What about UDI?'

'UDI?' Tim was scornful. 'He can't be serious.'

CHAPTER TWELVE

Tim was wrong. Before his meeting began Sir Huw would have jumped at any chance quietly to drop his campaign. But half an hour's talk with the 'Government of All the Talents' convinced him that UDI was not only desirable: it was necessary.

The Bull's Head at Beauville, where he had arranged the meeting between the representatives of the Talents with ap Coch, Siethenyn Pritchard and Twdr Plas Drynkin, always had a calming effect on him. Beauville has a sophisticated air, unique on the island. It's Gallic name was a heritage from Edward I who built one of his finest castles there. It has its own Mayor and Corporation and for centuries has argued for a restitution of its place as capital of the island. In Regency times it had been a fashionable watering place and it retains an air of genteel elegance. There was a pier which the council had wisely never allowed to fall into disrepair. During the 'fifties and 'sixties when the councils at other resorts had let these magnificent Victorian 'follies' rust and crumble, the pier at Beauville had been kept sound and spruce. By 1985 it was one of very few left in Wales. It became a listed building and was awarded an annual conservation grant. Visitors came to see it from all over Britain and stayed to make Beauville the most prosperous town on the island.

There was no promenade in the accepted sense of that word and certainly there were no hot dog stands. Manicured lawns swept down to the sea wall from a classic Georgian crescent of houses and a superior hotel.

Across the straits the mountains beyond Cader Idris made an endlessly changing picture. Behind the Georgian façade cobbled streets of pastel painted ancient houses, shoulder to shoulder, shuffled down side streets like switchbacks to the High Street.

The 'Bull', as it was universally called, had served beer without a break since the twelfth century. The original ale house, a small, narrow room, was still in use as an overflow bar, but over the years the inn had grown into a notable coaching house. During the Civil War it had been the headquarters of the Royalist troops. Dr Johnson had stayed there, Dickens, too, and, it was thought, Dean Swift and Thackeray. In the eighteenth century judges who came to the town on circuit made it their headquarters. Suffused with the benevolence that the Bull's home-brewed beer induced, their judgments had been erratic, and felons frequently found themselves freed when they had expected transportation. The beer which was still served there was of the order that Beaumont and Fletcher no doubt had in mind when they made one of their characters say 'Here's ale would make a cat speak'.

The others were already sampling it when ap Gryfydd arrived. Siethenyn, indeed, showed every sign of having been sampling it since the Bull had opened.

ap Gryfydd happily accepted a foaming pint in the pewter tankard he kept behind the bar, took a long satisfying pull at its contents and called the meeting to order.

The co-opted members of the Talents were represented by Tom Fort, the tycoon who had suggested ways of developing the island's economy, and Mr Justice Canter, a retired Colonial judge of great age. Mr Canter, though shrivelled by the years and hot climates, still wore suits which had covered the greater girth of his prime. Now they resembled nothing so much as a carapace. With his drawn neck stretching through a wing collar several sizes too large, topped by a reptilian face behind enormous glasses which was constantly moving from side to side, he looked like an elderly tortoise.

Twdr Plas Drynkin sat next to him, eyes wide with wonder, like a child before whom a vision of a fair country had been revealed. As, indeed, it had.

'I've been telling Plas Drynkin about the commercial possibilities of UDI,' Tom explained.

'Bloody revelation, man,' sighed Twdr. 'Sitting on a gold mine, we are. All that off-shore banking. Equal to a twenty pence rate, man.'

'A florin rate,' Siethenyn reminded him. 'Goin' off the

metric, don't forget. Sell coins to collectors. Another fortune.'

'Yes, but can it work?' asked ap Coch. 'I think we ought to have the judge's view. We've got to be sure of the legality of the position before we can hope to attract investment.' He turned to Mr Justice Canter. 'What is the position vis-à-vis international courts?'

Thus addressed, Mr Canter cleared his throat, a sound resembling the rattling of a half-empty box of matches.

'It raises,' he said at last, 'some rather nice points of law.'

He paused to make sure he had the attention of his audience and then continued.

'The highest tribunal is, of course, the International Court of Justice which is the legal arm of the United Nations.'

'Sounds just the ticket,' interrupted Siethenyn Accountant, only to be silenced by a severe glance from the judge.

'I'm afraid not. Under the rules of jurisdiction at the International Court only states may be parties in cases before the court.'

'But surely Tad IS a state now?' asked Twdr, who saw merchant bankers, laden with gold, flying out of every window.

'Alas, no. I have to tell you that only those states which were parties to the Statute may be so designated. You have not, in my understanding, aspired to membership of the United Nations?'

'Not yet,' admitted Twdr. 'But we're members of the County Councils Association. Fully paid up.'

'Not quite the same thing, I fear. Though there is provision that states non members of the UN may become parties to the Statute. But only in conditions which are determined afresh in each case by the General Assembly, upon the recommendation of the Security Council.

'There exists here the precedent of Switzerland,' the judge was musing now. 'In 1946, as I recall, the Federal Government sought to find out how Switzerland, though not a member of UNO, could become a party to the Statute of the Court. It was the decision of the Security Council that Switzerland could become a party on three conditions.'

'What are they?' broke in Twdr, who would have agreed to almost any condition which tethered the Merchant Bankers.

'Firstly you would have to accept its provisions.'

'We would, we would,' Twdr assured him.

'That would mean accepting the obligations of a member of the United Nations and undertaking to contribute to the expenses of the Court a sum of money to be decided by the General Assembly. And that is likely to involve you in a formidable expense.' There followed a series of strangled little noises which it took some time before the others identified as laughter. 'Even allowing for the golden prospects of Plas Drynkin's debut in the world of international banking.'

Satisfied at the reception of his jest the judge continued.

'No. It may be you would be able to get recognition in Europe and then, if necessary, you can apply to the Court under the terms of the trusteeship which Britain already holds in respect of Togoland and the Cameroons. I was for some time a Commissioner for Togoland. I well remember . . .'

'The Common Market Court,' supplied ap Coch, fearful of the judge's reputation for extended digression, 'do tell us about that.'

'Of course.' With an effort Mr Canter made the return trip from Togoland. 'The Court of Justice of the European Community springs from unlikely loins. It was, in fact, the child of the courts established after the Second World War by the European Coal and Steel Community and the European Atomic Energy Authority. Ah, thank you . . .' He broke off to acknowledge Siethenyn's gesture offering a refill of his empty glass. 'Perhaps, if I may, a dry sherry.'

Replenished, he took tortoise sips and, reinvigorated, continued.

'The European Court in Luxembourg was set up to ensure the observation of treaties, secondary legislation, the laws which the Court has itself created and the general principles of international law. It is not, I must warn you, the guardian of national law.' He glared at them sternly through his spectacles, which had, of course, tortoise-shell rims, seeking out any such misapprehension. None found, he continued.

'The Court is not the guardian of national law,' he repeated, 'and I fear it is on these grounds that the United Kingdom would almost certainly succeed in rebutting your application to appear before it.'

'So that horse won't run,' ap Gryfydd said flatly. 'And that's the end of it.'

'Not necessarily,' the judge told him. 'There are difficulties but there is yet a ray of hope.'

'And that is?' ap Gryfydd perked up.

'Well, the Court can penetrate what we lawyers have learned to call "the legal wall" of any member state of the EEC. And individuals and enterprises in member states do have limited rights to bring proceedings.'

'Hurrah,' said Siethenyn, who had been following the ups and downs of the conversation with some difficulty.

'Your huzzahs are a little premature. You would have to show an imbalance between the conflicting objectives of due administration and the patent need to annul an illegal act.'

'That's it, then,' said Siethenyn, 'isn't it?'

'Not necessarily. Under Articles 167 to 171 individuals or enterprises may not take proceedings against a member state.'

'Had it then, have we?' asked Twdr.

'Again, not necessarily,' the judge reproved. 'Under Articles 173 to 176 individuals *can* ask for the review of the legality of Community Action.'

'Would it work?'

'Not necessarily.'

'I'm completely lost,' ap Gryfydd admitted. 'Isn't there anything we can do that won't cost a fortune and take the rest of my limited lifetime?'

'Of course there is,' said the judge with an air of surprise at the question. 'Your approach can be through a UK court which is empowered to refer to the United Nations and then the International Court for a ruling.'

'And there are no snags? You see something is worrying me,' confessed ap Gryfydd. 'There's apparently some

London bigwig on the island and he came up on the same train as Will Looms Lloyd George's Auntie Megan. And she overheard him say that we couldn't win because the Court has no power over Britain.'

'Crudely put, but essentially correct,' the judge agreed. 'It has limited powers of enforcement and a member state is not forced to accept its ruling.'

'Oh.'

'But you are standing, don't forget, at the bar of public opinion. And, especially in the light of recent publicity, I would venture the view that Britain would not pursue that particular hare.'

'You think we've got a chance then?'

'An excellent chance. If I might venture to suggest the line which you might take?'

'Please do.'

'Very well. The charter of Henry IV says, does it not, that it is a condition of your sovereignty that you should always – what was the phrase? Ah, yes, I have it. "You should always do the king's purpose in time of war." It would seem to me that this condition is amply met by your distinguished record in World War Two. I should be happy to look into this further on your behalf.'

In the Land Rover going home ap Gryfydd was jubilant.

'There's only one thing, though,' he admitted to ap Coch. 'Why on earth couldn't he have told us about applying through the British courts in the first place? Saved hours.'

'Nature of the beast,' ap Coch explained. 'Lawyers never do. Part of the mystique. Everyone does it. No one likes to make his job seem too easy. Try putting your car in a garage and then ask them what they've done. Never understand a damn word. I'm glad, though, we're not going to the Community Court. Make it rather bad form to ask their help then chuck the EEC. Still, I reckon it was a pretty rewarding evening.'

'Indeed, yes.' In the back Twdr sighed ecstatically. He had arrived with Siethenyn, but no one ever returned from the Bull as Siethenyn's passenger. 'Off-shore banking, man. Bloody revelation!'

'Don't forget Sunday opening, boy,' interrupted Siethenyn sleepily. Wisely he, too, had decided to return with ap Gryfydd. He'd succumbed to Twdr's argument that it gave him an excuse to go back to the Bull to collect his car.

It had been a rewarding evening, thought ap Gryfydd. He saw a new golden age of prosperity dawning. Ceri's chances of talking him out of UDI were zero. Home Rule for Tad was now a number one priority.

'Right,' he said at last. 'Plas Drynkin. Would you be so kind as to draw up a feasibility study based on what Tom Fort told you? And you, Alun, could you liaise with the judge and set the machinery in motion for getting on the Court's lists?'

His forces disposed and the detailed administration satisfactorily accepted by the others, he was all benevolence.

'Might as well call in at the Groeslon for a nightcap. Ask you back but Ceri's home.'

'No more for me,' said Siethenyn virtuously. 'I'm driving.'

'No, you're not, you bloody idiot,' said Twdr. 'You're a passenger, man.'

'Oh well, in that case . . .'

CHAPTER THIRTEEN

'But Sir Pelham, are you determined? I scarcely think your presence on the island among scenes of violent debauchery is consonant with your dignity as a senior representative of HMG.'

Tim was puzzled. He had lapsed into Whitehall Mandarin as a last resort. Effyngham-Blynd was, he knew, a fifth generation coward. Yet he was determined not to leave the island. It was very odd. Tim would have taken short odds that the lurid description he had just given him of the *Cwcwll* would have had Sir Pelham reaching for his suitcase. But his chief refused even to consider returning to London.

'One thinks you are taking an unnecessarily pessimistic view,' he told his astonished junior. 'One cannot believe that the forthcoming festival is anything other than an interesting survival. One will watch it with a great deal of interest.'

'You're going to watch it?' Tim could scarcely have been more surprised had Sir Pelham announced that he intended to strip to his lavender undervest and pants and throw himself into the heart of the battling scrum of villagers.

He looked at his chief. In the privacy of his room Sir Pelham had cast off his formal jacket and waistcoat, which now hung primly in his wardrobe. Surprisingly he had changed into a striking shantung dressing gown in vertical stripes of black and gold. He looked for all the world like an overweight, out of condition honey-bee and the aroma of pungent unguent hung in the air.

He might almost have been waiting for a woman, thought Tim wonderingly. Certainly he looked disappointed when he opened the door and found me outside.

'Of course one will watch it.'

'But Sir Pelham. Only think. Pig's head broth.'

He was relieved to see a shudder like jostled custard animate the other man.

'One will, of course, lunch out. One assumes the island does have restaurants?'

'I suppose so,' Tim rejoined weakly. 'Though they may be closed, of course. It's by way of being a local holiday.'

'What day isn't? To judge by the number of persons in the bar at lunchtime there are 365 of them. The island seems to be permanently *en fête*.'

'There is a dangerous euphoria in the air, Permanent Secretary. It merely reinforces the view, which I feel I must put to you, that your presence here tomorrow night, to put it at its strongest, will be incendiary. And it does seem to me that since Sir Huw will not be able to see you for another two days your position might be said to be equivocal.'

It was quite the wrong choice of words. Tim was a creature of his time. The subtleties of Mandarin were really beyond him.

'Equivocal?' Sir Pelham boomed, his eyebrows soaring. 'You make one sound like the king's mistress,' he added coyly.

Tim hurried to correct himself. 'Not at all, Permanent Secretary. It did just seem that since you have examined the situation on the ground you might just consider returning to London to write an interim report and await developments.'

Plainly Sir Pelham was tempted. His club, his comfortable chambers, the cosseting of his staff, were all pleading in his heart for him to quit this barbaric island and this punitive hotel. But something stronger was bidding him stay. For a moment he was silent and then, making his mind up all at once, he leaned forward and *sotto voce* confided in his young assistant.

'It's a matter of oranges,' he admitted at last.

'Oranges???'

'Yes. Umm. Oranges.'

'But Sir Pelham. We can buy oranges anywhere. They have superb oranges on Euston Station. I'll gladly get you a bag.'

Oddly Sir Pelham was exhibiting what in anyone else would have indicated extreme embarrassment.

'To be more specific. An Orange.'

In a moment Tim knew all. When Sir Pelham made the story of Mary-Anne's Orange known to him the young man understood at once the strength of the cord which bound his Head of Department to Byndrynkin.

'Of course, it's all quite silly. But one does not wish to offend the dear, simple soul. One has every reason to believe that One is to be the recipient. Certain indications have been made. No pledge, you understand. But one flatters oneself one has made an impression,' Sir Pelham confided archly.

Well, that explains the dressing gown and pomade, Tim told himself. The old sly-boots was lobbying.

Tim had been in the Civil Service long enough to know that the consuming passion of his seniors was the pursuit of Honours. To outsiders the yearning for what had once been orders of chivalry and were now debased into the Service's equivalent of company perks, might have seemed bizarre. But Tim knew that it was the force which drove them. Sir Pelham was acting out a Pavlovian response. Mary-Anne's orange had become An Honour. And if the orange was the only Honour to be had on the island Sir Pelham was determined not to go home without it. Even if it meant swimming through a sea of pig's head broth or exposing himself to a biting Force Eight gale on the seashore, watching the morrow's massacre. Sir Pelham hated the sight of blood but Greater Issues were at stake. Sir Pelham was determined to be One of the Boys.

Tim wondered how far his boss was prepared to stoop to become a Companion of the Orange First Class. The next sentence told him.

'Come, my boy,' Sir Pelham said. 'Shall we venture down to the bar? One would so enjoy a nightcap. And might it not be a wise plan to let the good people here see one with one's hair, as it were, down? One is aware that one is too often seen by the labouring classes in one's patrician role. We might share a convivial glass of port, though I feel it may be of modest vintage. The rustic palate is easily pleased. Dinner, though adequate, was scarcely *haute cuisine*.'

Tim, who had dined satisfyingly on fish and chips on the way back from Plas Becod, thought the island catering admirable. He now felt a reprehensible desire to cause his insufferable senior pain.

'I'm afraid it's not vintage at all, Permanent Secretary,' he told him cruelly. 'In fact it's Australian.'

The bolt struck home. Sir Pelham winced, but the fleeting spasm was soon brought under control.

'My dear boy,' he rallied gamely, 'when in Rome . . .'

But some faint doubt still nibbled at him. As they walked down the corridor towards the staircase which would take them to the bar he paused and took Tim's arm.

'Er. Did you get the paper you ordered this morning?' he asked hesitantly.

'Oh yes,' said Tim. '*The Times*.'

Sir Pelham was puzzled and disconcerted

'How very odd. I ordered *The Times*, of course. But clearly there was some break down in communication and I received someone else's order.'

'Oh? What paper did you get?'

'The *Farmer and Stockbreeder*. Obviously meant for someone else.'

'But, Sir Pelham, there are no other guests. Only us.'

'That's very singular,' said Sir Pelham crossly.

'I'll take it up with the management,' said Tim, but Sir Pelham stopped him hurriedly.

'By no means. It might rebound on that poor chambermaid. One would not wish that. Have you met her, by any chance?'

'No, not really. Something small and bent came scurrying into my room, muttering something in Welsh, but I'm afraid I took no notice of it.'

'Such a pity,' Sir Pelham told him with an air of considerable satisfaction. 'One engaged her for quite some time in friendly conversation. One flatters oneself one made quite an impression. Quite an impression. Ah, here is the dear lady now.'

He paused and raised his hands rather in the manner of saints on ikons, his progress momentarily halted. Mary-Anne, whose powers of materialisation had no equal in the psychic world, appeared from a shadowy alcove. Checked, for a second, at the sight of the two civil servants, she then propelled herself, with a whirring of corset bones, into the centre of the corridor. The cackle factory in her throat went into overtime, her freckled, skeletal hands tightened on her mop and bucket, which combined together in an ominous roll, and she moved towards them at a geriatric trot.

'Good evening, dear lady,' boomed Sir Pelham. 'Still busily engaged about your duties, I see. Oh excellent woman! If only there were more like you in the world! Such a sense of responsibility! Oh, such a blessing!'

His words, or rather the resonant boom which echoed down the corridor, had an astonishing effect on Mary-Anne Orange. Not even the most sycophantic pursuer of her orange had ever been able to bring himself to compliment her quite so fulsomely before. On her first meeting she had not been impressed by Sir Pelham, which explained the *Farmer and Stockbreeder*. For one thing she had been unable to understand a word he had said to her. And he smelled of scent. She understood very little of what he said now but he had blessed her. And in the resonant tones of a revivalist preacher. No one had ever blessed Mary-Anne Orange before. Roman Catholics on the island crossed themselves nervously as she passed and the Chapel Elder had frequently taken her to task for her attachment to milk stout.

'A preacher, for sure,' some little voice in her mind chided her. 'And you givin' 'im the *Farmer and Stockbreeder*?' The magazine was pretty heavy artillery in Mary-Anne's battery. 'There's shame on you, girl. And him a Man of God.' An even darker voice whispered: 'And such a fine set up Man of God, too.' And a still darker one whispered to her to try and get a sight of him in his pyjamas. For, it must be sadly confessed, that the skeleton of lust still rattled in her ancient mind. Lights long dimmed flickered fitfully in her rheumy eye. Her heart, like a wrinkled hazelnut left over from a long departed Christmas, lurched and made a tentative but plucky somersault. Emotions suffused a sandpaper skin long dead to their touch. Her body was sending signals so arcane her brain could scarcely decipher them. Love, never fastidious, had touched the heart of Mary-Anne Orange.

'The voice of a preacher,' she muttered wonderingly. And a preacher who saw her worth! She could hardly prevent herself from falling at his feet. Only the realisation of the absolute impossibility of regaining her feet once down deterred her. She made up her mind at once. She would shower this great man with oranges. Together they would dance, he in his Wyncyette pyjamas, she in her shift, down a perspective of orange boxes, for the idea that oranges ever grew on trees in groves was too bizarre a notion for her to accommodate. They came in boxes from the Half Moon Stores. But there was something she must do first. A wrong must be righted. With a whispered endearment that came out sounding remarkably like a curse, she once again shuddered with emotion and went chugging down the corridor for all the world like a toy tin boat propelled at the stern by camphor tablets. And the odour of moth balls she left in her wake enhanced the image.

Sir Pelham's benediction followed her.

'Good night, dear Miss Orange,' he called. And then in quite a different tone remarked to Tim: 'What curious surnames these people do have.'

Tim was disgusted at Sir Pelham's blatant insincerity. But when he retired to his room later that night in pleasant anticipation of an hour with *The Times*' crossword he was furious. For the newspaper had been removed. In its place lay the *Farmer and Stockbreeder*.

The evening had not been a success. At the foot of the staircase four silent men were playing dominoes, their great, chapped, red hands clutching the bones with ease; in the case of one giant a massive palm covering them entirely. Tim had never seen a man of his size. Seated hunched over the table, he still appeared to be standing upright. Though none of his companions were tall, they were dwarfed by the fourth man. His free hand completely masked the pint pot from which he frequently drank in deep draughts and equally frequently replenished by rapping it on the counter and relinquishing it only when another full one appeared at its side. During the exchange not a word was spoken.

'Doesn't say much, does he?' Tim ventured to the man at

his side. He was a small man with a bald, domed Martian-like head. He was dressed incongruously in a well-cut but threadbare black overcoat with a velvet collar. Tim noticed that the cuffs were frayed and the trousers underneath it were the width of the fashion of the 'fifties. His black, horn-rimmed spectacles were bound at the bridge with electrician's insulating tape in a violent shade of green.

'Doesn't have to, does he?' the voice was soft and sibilant. 'Evans Cae Pant, that is. Captain of *Cwcwll*, man. Ex-SAS.'

'Doesn't seem to pay either.'

'No, well. Tradition, see. Game winners don't pay for beer.'

'But the game isn't till tomorrow.'

'Don't make no difference. Bound to win. Always does, see. Last year two of the fishermen wouldn't let go of the *Cwcwll*. So he brought them too. *Arglwydd*, they were mad, I'll tell you.'

'I suppose he'd have to pay for tonight's beer after the game if he lost.'

'*Diawl*, no. If the fishermen got it to their pub he'd just go and get it back.'

'On his own?'

'Well, no. The others would go, of course. But there wouldn't be much for them to do, fair play.'

'It sounds a very rough game.'

'Rough? Not really. Not had a fatality for years, man.'

'I don't suppose you take part?'

'Not take part? Not take part? I am *Ffwl*, the Fool, man. It's my hat they burn. Can't start the game without it.'

'But don't you get burned yourself?'

'Every year,' the little man told him proudly. 'Blisters the size of duck eggs.'

'But why on earth do you do it, if it's so dangerous?'

The little man looked at him with something like contempt.

'Tradition, man.'

'I suppose it would be more dangerous if you, forgive me, had more hair.'

'Burned off when I was twenty-one, man,' the little man boasted. 'Bloody Kojak? Not in the race.'

Sir Pelham meanwhile was having trouble with the barman, John King.

'No, I do not want lemonade in my port,' he was saying firmly. 'I prefer it neat.'

''Oo does he think he is?' muttered John to the others. 'Bloody John Wayne. He'll be breaking crisps with his bare hands next, see if he won't.'

Unused as they were to Sir Pelham's Civil Service uniform of black coat and striped trousers, many of the customers had taken him for a superior undertaker. With the warm interest that all Celts take in death and its ceremonial a lady with orange hair and an ex-WD overcoat edged over to him.

'Over on a bit of business, then, is it?' she asked him respectfully.

'In a manner of speaking,' Sir Pelham replied grandly.

'There's a pity,' said the orange-red hair with quiet satisfaction. ''Oo's gone, then? Not prying. I got a professional reason for asking.'

'Gone? Gone where?'

The lady with the orange-red hair raised her eyes to the ceiling.

'Up there, I hope,' she said. 'Never speak ill of the dead. Come on, you can tell me. I lays them out. Always have.' Then, sharply: 'That Mair hasn't been in taking my business, has she?'

'I've no idea what you're talking about, madam.' Sir Pelham was completely nonplussed. And when he saw that, unaccountably, his words were making his companion very angry he backed away in alarm.

'She has, has she? Bloody old *gwrach*, that one. No right to be touching. Corpses is mine. And my mam's before me. Doesn't wash 'em proper, y'know. And don't leave anything in their pockets. No, nor no rings neither. She'll 'ave 'em off their fingers soon as look. Goin' to place a little ladder in the coffin, then?'

'Coffin, madam?' cried Sir Pelham in alarm. 'Little ladder? What can you mean?'

'New to the business, is it?' said the lady with orange hair. 'Thought so. Or you'd never 'ave 'ad that Mair layin' out. Well, let me tell you, Glyn Coffin always puts a ladder in with them. Real oak. No messing with Glyn Coffin. Not a splinter of pine anywhere. Real sateen he uses, too.'

'Madam, I fear you labour under a misapprehension. What can you think one is?'

'Undertaker, aren't you? Not from here, though, or I'd 'ave known you. Caernarfon, is it? I don't believe you're even Welsh. Good God. Fancy havin' yourself touched by a bloody *Sais*. You'll not get near me, I'll tell you.'

'My good woman, I don't want to touch you. And I am certainly not an undertaker.'

'Why you dressed up like one, then?' This accusingly.

'I am not dressed up like one.'

'Don't shout, there's a good man,' advised the barman. 'We don't want no trouble.'

'It's the port, you know,' he told the customers, who had been attracted by the raised voices. 'Drinking it neat, see. Wouldn't take a drop of lemonade. Asked him particular.'

Sir Pelham was near tears.

'I don't like lemonade.'

'I do,' chimed in one of the customers, a wrinkled old lady in a balding fur coat, hinting firmly but in vain. 'Nothing to touch a drop of port and lemon.'

'And I am *not* an undertaker.' He was almost screaming now. 'I am a civil servant.'

At his words the whole bar fell silent. Even the barman backed off in alarm. The lady with the orange hair looked at him with horror.

'Good God!' she said. 'Social Security! A bloody snooper!' And grabbing her drink she hurried away to the far end of the bar. Not even Dracula could have produced a similar reaction. As other customers moved unobtrusively away Sir Pelham was left in an ever widening empty circle. As though in a nightmare a raucous cackling broke out. Mary-Anne Orange was peering over the balcony.

'Casting out the Sinners,' she muttered, waving her arms over her head. 'Go at it, man. Give 'em stick, Preacher. Tell

’em they’ll all go to ’ell. But not Mary-Anne Orange. I got a nice *Times* for you. Mary-Anne knows.’

In the stunned silence Tim detached himself from his new acquaintance. He moved to Sir Pelham’s side.

‘Better turn in perhaps, sir? Bit of a misunderstanding.’

‘Yes, that’s best,’ said the barman. ‘Nasty that port on its own. You have a nice lie down.’

Sir Pelham permitted himself to be led from the bar. And not even the sight of *The Times* on his counterpane had the power to soothe him.

Tim returned briefly to the bar.

‘Excuse me,’ he said to the barman, who was looking at him warily, ‘I thought I’d put your mind at rest. We’re not Social Security. We’re to do with Planning.’

The relief was palpable.

‘There now,’ said the barman, raising a glass to thc optic, ‘have this on me.’

Tim accepted.

‘Tell me,’ he said, ‘why do you put little ladders in the coffins with the dead?’

The barman looked at him in surprise.

‘So they can climb up to heaven, of course,’ he said.

‘Of course,’ said Tim. ‘How silly of me not to realise.’

And it was then that he decided that one day, come hell or high water, he was going to live on Tad.

CHAPTER FOURTEEN

Before going to bed Tim had telephoned Ceri to warn her of Sir Pelham's intention to attend the *Gêm*. Unfortunately the telephone was answered by Sir Huw who was sufficiently exercised by the voice of a strange young man to eavesdrop unashamedly on Ceri's end of the conversation which followed.

Ceri was not surprised. She had long accepted her father's proprietorial interest in other people's telephone calls, letters, indeed any communication to the Plas. It would have been foolhardy to keep a diary at Plas Becod and from long practice she automatically edited her answers on the telephone. The years had taught her to be circumspect. Sir Huw was equal to that. Circumspection was alien to him. If he did not understand anything, then he asked.

'What was all that about?' he growled when at last the call ended and a thoughtful Ceri put down the receiver.

'Sorry?' she asked absently.

'The phone call. What was it about?'

'Don't pry, daddy. It was private.'

'I am not prying,' Sir Huw insisted. 'When a strange young man telephones my daughter in the middle of the night . . .'

'It's a quarter to eleven. Or 22.45 Eurotime, if you prefer it.'

'I do not prefer it,' roared Sir Huw. Eurotime had been officially introduced in 1982 and was widely used everywhere except on the two islands. 'I will not have Frog-time in my house. And I won't have young men ringing you up until they have been properly introduced.'

'Oh, don't be tiresome, daddy. Anyway, he has.'

'Has what?'

'Been introduced. He was here, earlier this evening.'

'Here? A strange young man? And you in the house on your own?'

'Yes. If you don't count eight servants.'

'I don't.' Sir Huw belonged to the same generation as the man who, dining with his wife and being waited on by a butler, two footmen and a maid, prefaced a remark by saying, 'Now we are alone . . .'.

'Anyway, it was you he wanted to see. It was hardly his fault if you were out playing Owain Glyndwr.'

'Me? What for?'

She decided to take the plunge.

'He's from Whitehall. And he was hoping to arrange a meeting between you and his principal, one Effyngham-Blynd.'

'F-ing and blinding in my house?' Sir Huw had been aware of the Whitehall presence since the two men had stepped off the London train at Bangor three nights before. But laying smoke screens was instinctive in him. 'In front of a young girl, scarcely out of her teens? I'll horsewhip the young dog.'

'Do listen. His principal is called Sir Pelham Effyngham-Blynd.'

'I don't believe it. No one could go through life with a name like that.'

'It is a bit of a facer,' Ceri admitted. 'But according to his assistant – his name's Tim Crisp, by the way, and he's very nice – according to Tim, if anyone had to have a name like that, giving it to Effyngham-Blynd was an act of divine justice. A tic of the first water, by all accounts.'

'Doesn't like his boss, then?' Sir Huw stored the information for future use. 'What does this Sir Whatever-his-name-is want?'

'He's a sort of emissary from the Secretary of State for Wales. He wants you to drop this UDI.'

Ignoring her father's derisive snort she went on.

'I do wish you'd see him and consider what he has to say. I'm sure they're ready to concede your points about the address and county status.'

'Very kind of them,' interrupted Sir Huw drily. 'Didn't say how they were going to prevent us, I suppose? Send in another force of commando policemen, perhaps?'

'Oh, daddy, I only want you to think about it. Make some

excuse so you don't have to see this man and give yourself time to consider. You could get into very serious trouble, you know. I'd hate to see you being carted off to Shrewsbury Gaol. Or the Tower of London, or wherever it is they take traitors.'

'Traitors! From you? I never thought I'd hear that word on your lips.'

'Oh, *I* don't think that, of course. But from their point of view, don't you see, that's what you are? And they will do everything they can to humiliate you and discredit you.'

She moved over to sit on the arm of her father's chair, kissing him fondly on the top of his head. 'I couldn't bear that. You're good and you're brave and you love these islands, I know. But, daddy, not even *you* can take on the British government.'

He thought for a moment, looking deep into the flames from the logs in the hearth and when he spoke his voice was unusually soft. All the theatrical gestures which made him a sort of stage squire and which he used with delight were gone.

'Listen to me, *cariad*,' he said. 'When I was fifty I decided I would never be serious again. Whatever happened, however bad it was, well, I wouldn't have to put up with it all that long. My life was two-thirds behind me; I'd seen some terrible things in the war and nothing could possibly be as bad as that again.

'Funny, you know, people keep telling me that I can't beat the government. It's too big, they say. Odd, really. Forty-five years ago a chap called Kennedy said the same thing about Britain. When France fell and it was only little Britain against all the power of Nazi Germany. He was the American ambassador in London then. Britain can't win, he said. Well, *Arglwydd*, we showed them then, didn't we?

'The only thing was we thought we were fighting for freedom. Freedom? Chap was telling me the other day that there are twenty-nine government departments that can send a man into your house without so much as a by-your-leave. Though, I'm bound to say, no one's tried it on here. The

Nazis did that, you know. Home or country, it didn't matter. Barge in. Just if it suited them.

'Well, for my money, the government is today's Nazis. Not as crude, of course. No gas ovens. But they still insist that everyone thinks and does things their way. Build a house, even a pigeon hut, that doesn't comply with their regulations and they'll pull it down round your ears. Planning regulations? Our ancestors didn't have planning regulations when they built Chester or York. Or the best parts of London, for that matter. Dammit, you couldn't build Bangor Cathedral today. The window space isn't the right size for the floor space behind it. Think of all those glorious medieval cities like Canterbury. Or a Georgian one like Bath. They were built before anyone had thought of governments interfering in the sort of houses you put up. And look at the dreadful things we've had since the end of the war. Gloomy municipal tower blocks. Identical city centres so that you don't know where you are until you buy a newspaper. If it's the *Daily Post* you're in Liverpool. If you come out with the *Yorkshire Post* you're either in Bradford, Leeds or Huddersfield.

'After the war Britain *was* a comfortable little country. Oh, a bit shabby and short of food. But it was easy living here. Like wearing a comfortable pair of slippers. There wasn't a lot of money about. But what there was bought a joint for most people's Sunday dinners. Ordinary people could still afford to take their families on holiday. Millions of men could go to their locals for the last hour and when they went home and closed their front doors they were in their own castles.

'Look at the place now. Crippling rates and taxes. And for what? To finance huge armies of bureaucrats in vast palaces. To pay for the junketings of Common Market MPs and our own parliamentarians, too. Though, God knows, they have less say in affairs now than we used to have on Merioneth County Council. Mind you, they were clever. Altered the money so that folk wouldn't notice that prices were going through the roof. I wonder how much that cost? And all the other changes that followed. The petrol pumps that had to be changed to sell petrol in litres. New measurements. And do you remember those damned yellow telephone boxes? And STD? Pouring millions into building factories in Scotland though businessmen warned then that they were siting them in the wrong part of the country and couldn't hope to succeed. They didn't do it to help the people, mark you. They were afraid they'd lose seats to the Scottish Nationalists if they didn't. And what happened? The factories ran at a loss for a few years and then closed. And the people were still as badly off. And what about the new counties? Millions of pounds wasted just to give MPs new constituencies that would ensure they kept their majorities. Little things, too. Remember in about 1980 when they closed the WI markets because the kitchens of the women who made home-made jam and so on didn't conform with some damned regulations? Home bakers went the same way. Oh, I know we got the WI markets back. But only because MPs wanted to have WI jam in the House of Commons canteen.

'Little things. But all of a sudden we were living in a different country from the one we'd fought for. It wouldn't be so bad if the quality of life had improved. But has it? England is an industrial waste land; Wales is worse. And why? Because there aren't enough votes to be had here to make it worth the government's while to help us.

'Dammit, it wouldn't be so bad if the bureaucrats could do the job. But they can't. Wine lakes, butter mountains, near as dammit wars over fishing rights and farm produce.'

It was a long speech for Sir Huw and he broke off to stab the dying fire with the broad sword that did duty as a poker.

'I tell you, we've lost almost every little freedom that mattered. Dammit, in '81 they even tried to tell me that my tenant farmers couldn't pass their farms on to their sons. I ignored them, of course. Damned if I was going to break up a tradition that has worked well for centuries.

'They don't understand, d'you see. Small farmers put in a fourteen-hour day, longer during lambing. Keeping the land in heart, getting up in the winter when it's still dark to look after the stock. Working like slaves. And what for? So they'll have something to hand over to their sons that's a little better than they got from their own fathers. And why d'you suppose sons worked for little more than their keep when they could be idling about on Social Security? Because one day the farm would be theirs. And what happens now on the mainland? Little farms have been joined up and sold to international companies that know nothing about the land and couldn't care a damn about it either.

'What do the bureaucrats know about life? Straight from school to university. Then out of university into their centrally heated offices. What can they know about land? Land's soil to them. For growing things in. It's more than that to us. Land's family. It's as much our kin as our brothers and sisters. It's a child to be nursed when it's sick and boasted about when it's doing well. It's the parent that provides our food. Aye, and our clothes and shelter too.

'Why, when I was a boy there were families round here that wouldn't set foot in a shop to buy food. Now look at them over there!' He jerked his head in the direction of the mainland. 'Bread like roofing felt and eating frozen food like so many bloody eskimoes. Damme, they even put red dye in the meat to make it look nice. Can you imagine? Red dye? *Arglwydd*, the world's gone mad.'

He put his hand over his daughter's which was resting on his shoulder.

'Oh, I know you think your old father's gone soft in the head. And I know everyone who reads about UDI thinks I'm just another dotty old Welshman. It's all a huge joke. But it isn't, *cariad*.

'That was how it started, *chwarae teg*. And there've been times when I wished I hadn't started it at all. But Tom Fort is no fool and he's been painting a picture tonight about these islands and the sort of life we could have here that's convinced me we're right to try for our freedom.

'And if we fail? Well, ap Coch reckons Shrewsbury Gaol, or the Tower of London, come to that, can't be as bad as some of the Jap prison camps he was in on the Kwai. And the beauty is, my girl, we can't entirely fail. Because if we've done nothing else we've made them think about freedom. The little but so very important freedoms that they are in danger of losing. If they haven't already lost them. Perhaps now when a new damn silly regulation comes in someone will question it. Because, believe me, girl, it's the little nibblers that gobble up freedom. Not the ones like Hitler who take huge bites and choke themselves. It's faceless ones who are the danger. Perhaps when people see what we've done on Tad, standing alone like Britain did during the war, perhaps then they'll have the heart put back into them. And the next time some jumped-up Jack-in-Office tells them they can't paint their houses blue or black or pink if they want, they'll say "Why not?". And if that is what being a traitor is, lovely girl, well then, I'm the biggest double-dyed traitor in the kingdom. And, by God, I'm proud of it.'

He waved the broad sword jubilantly, hacking at imaginary bureaucrats.

'And, dammit, you can bet the government'll think twice before they do any more interfering with our freedom. Fellows like your friend F-ing and Blinding won't feel quite so safe in their office chairs.'

Ceri had never known her father so eloquent or so serious. She looked at him now with a new respect.

'Oh, daddy,' she said, 'I didn't know.'

Her father looked up at her, eyes twinkling.

'Old Dai had lived a terrible life and when he died he fell straight to the bottom of the fiery pit. And when he looked up he saw God looking down at him over the edge. "Oh Big Man," he said, "I didn't know." "*Chwarae teg*," said God, "you know now."

'Now, off to bed with you. It's the *Gêm* tomorrow. A big day. You'll need your rest.'

At the door Ceri paused.

'There's just one thing. That phone call. Tim says Sir Pelham is coming to the *Gêm*. You won't do anything silly, will you?'

'Silly? Me?' her father replied innocently. 'Certainly not. And it's Tim now, is it? Haven't fallen for him, have you?'

And because of the haste with which she denied it her father knew that she had.

'It's just that this Sir Pelham is so devious,' she went on.

'Don't worry your head about that. Good God, girl,

deviousness was invented in Wales. We draw it in with our mother's milk. Coming to the *Gêm*, is he? Well, we'll just have to make sure it's a day to remember for him, won't we?'

That night Sir Huw sat up late by the fire deep in thought. From time to time slow smiles chased themselves across his face like summer breezes. Finally he went into his business room and made a number of telephone calls. At last, satisfied, he made his way to bed. He was still smiling happily long after he fell asleep.

Across the island Effyngham-Blynd's sleep had been less than seraphic. His brush with what he thought of as the brutish peasantry had thoroughly unmanned him. Fright stayed with him like a daunting nurse at his bedside, even after he fell asleep. His dreams were filled with tribes of orange-haired women, streaked with woad and dressed in skins. Screaming and brandishing huge clubs they had pursued him up endless hills and down valleys which went on for ever. In his mind they had become confused with those Druid hand-maidens of whom Tacitus had written. The women who had danced, wild-haired, on the shores of Anglesey, putting fear into the hearts of a Roman legion.

Matters were not improved when he was dragged from his slumbers by a rough shaking. When he opened startled eyes the nightmare seemed to have pursued him into wakefulness. Only inches from his own face was that of Mary-Anne Orange, leering at him.

'Wha . . . wha . . . wha . . .' was as much as he could manage.

'Wake up, your reverence,' said the lady, patting him now on his Wyncyetted shoulder. 'Brought you a cup of tea, I have. And the nice *Times* for you, see. Went for it myself.'

Limply Sir Pelham took the tea and watched with growing satisfaction as she darted round the room disarranging everything she touched. Normally he would have objected. But the Orange was paramount. It was in the bag, surely? It was his. He knew it. A great warm glow of satisfaction suffused him.

Alas, it was the last he was to experience for some time.

CHAPTER FIFTEEN

Gêm Cwcwll is Tad's equivalent of the FA cup. When Sir Pelham, with a worried Tim at his side, made an apprehensive appearance, the causeway which ran along the head of the Red Beach and the metalled road which ran behind it were thronged with people.

It was a bitterly cold morning, yet bathed in brilliant sunshine and the hard, gem-like quality of the light brought out every detail of the day as though etched on copper. In the cold air conversations froze into balloons of air the moment they left the mouths of their speakers so that the scene looked like drawings from an inspired comic strip. Ears that escaped from under striped, knitted woollen caps, each with an identical bobble, were instantly nipped for their temerity by the ever watchful frost.

Everyone was there. Sir Huw was seated in a throne-like chair in the back of his Land Rover while Grout huddled in the driving seat, duffle-coated and looking like an overweight goblin. Next to Sir Huw's 'throne' stood an empty smaller chair and at his feet was a modest electric fire which had been recklessly attached to the battery. Under the bonnet a large can of soup was wedged under the manifold to heat. To keep up the heat of the can and the strength of the battery Grout had left the engine running. Periodically he heartened it with stabs at the accelerator pedal. This produced a dragon-like roar from the engine and a belch of belligerent smoke from the exhaust. Both smoke and roar served to isolate the Land Rover. Anyone who wanted to talk to Sir Huw – and many did – waited outside the range of the exhaust, then darted through the clearing smoke to the side of the truck. Sir Huw was in fine form. Frequent pulls on an immense brandy flask were making him impervious both to the cold and to the disturbance his vehicle was causing. Occasionally he would roar out a greeting which rose above the noise of the exhaust.

'That's Sir Huw over there,' whispered Tim, pointing him out.

'Good God,' said Sir Pelham, awed in spite of himself. 'Looks like Piltdown Man,' he added as he took in the lowering, bearded figure, the wild hair crammed into an ancient deer-stalker, its flaps struggling to contain ears like elongated radar dishes.

The lean, elegant figure of ap Coch appeared in the cloud of exhaust smoke which he ignored as he climbed over the tail of the truck and settled himself into the empty seat at Sir Huw's side.

'And that's his agent, Colonel ap Coch.'

Other figures emerged dramatically from the smoke and Tim ticked them off as they appeared. First came four men in a body ranging themselves at the tailboard, feudal sub-chiefs paying homage.

'Those are the Druids. They're a sort of war council. That's Twdr Plas Drynkin, then there's Siethenyn and Glyn Pritchard, Meredith Bread Rolls . . .' Tim identified them all, managing to mispronounce every single name.

'And who, in God's name, is the little one? The one in the cap who looks as though he's been blown off a quarry face?'

'That's Eddi Pant Ddu,' said Tim. 'He's a cousin of Mary-Anne Orange.'

Sir Pelham's interest lasered.

'Really? A most striking man. One must contrive to have a word.'

'Actually, they're all cousins of Mary-Anne Orange.'

'What, all four?'

'Everyone who's here today, I should imagine,' Tim told him.

'Even that curious lady with the knitting bag? The one who is apparently made of string?'

'Oh, no, that's Miss Magersfontein-Blair. She's the archivist. The lady who found the charter that started the whole thing.'

'Lady?' Sir Pelham's eyebrows hurled themselves into the rim of his homburg. 'Looks more like a runaway rope.'

In truth there was something of the cordwainer in Miss

Magersfontein-Blair's appearance. The polo neck of an Arran sweater had escaped far enough from the embrace of innumerable cardigans to wrap itself round the lower half of her face.

'One can only hope that she and Sir Huw never breed,' Sir Pelham observed. 'Genetically speaking it would set the race back a thousand years.'

Snug in a fetching après-ski track suit Ceri now made an appearance. Tim's voice softened. 'Ah, that's Sir Huw's daughter, Ceri. A charming girl.'

He was rewarded with a piercing glance from Sir Pelham.

Across the crowd two other men watched in isolation. On a grassy knoll Gareth Jenkyn shivered in an ancient mackintosh at the side of Meredith ap Owen in a pristine sheepskin coat and a fur hat. His smart cavalry twill trousers were tucked into fleecy-lined sheepskin boots. He looked deliberately medieval and he was enjoying himself hugely.

He extended a gloved and sheep-skinned arm in a gesture which took in all the jostling crowds. Enterprising tradesmen had set up booths. One was doing a roaring trade in steaming cups of broth, a second dispensed portions of jellied eels from a vast tin bath. Incongruously, pizzas were being baked in a makeshift oven made of bricks by the ever resourceful staff of Meredith Bread Rolls. Next to his booth Will Looms Lloyd George was handing out pots of ale drawn from massive barrels at the rear of the beer tent.

'Just like the Middle Ages, boy,' sighed Meredith. 'Must have been like this before that devil Edward I swept down with his Saxon hordes. Crushed the soul of our great Celtic nation under the heels of the English army.'

But Gareth was cold and in no mood for romantic visions.

'An army of sixteen thousand', he reminded Meredith cruelly, 'of which nine thousand were Welshmen.'

In the tiny dark cave where his soul lurked he hoarded up the crestfallen look which his gibe produced. Gareth now stood in the shattered remnants of a dream, scattered at his feet in glisters of coloured glass.

'Fair play. They were South Walians,' he countered with

little hope. 'Always against us, the South Walians.'

Gareth sadistically pressed home his advantage.

'And Lloyd George was born in Manchester and you and Saunders Lewis are both Scousers,' he jibed.

'Accidents of birth,' Gareth had really wounded his fellow conspirator now. 'Doesn't affect our patriotism. We're both from Welsh family backgrounds.'

Gareth brushed a rat's tail of hair out of his eye and smoothed it back where the rest was apparently awaiting an oil change.

'When will you realise that the war is an international one. You can never hope to win your nation back until all over the world the forces of capital are in disarray. Divide and rule. The bloody *Sais* were at it even in Edward's day. And the amazing thing is that you help them. North Wales versus South Wales, Wales versus England. It's not the bloody World Cup, you know. Oh, what's the use? What time is the demonstration?'

'Should have been on its way by now. Timed to coincide with the start of the game. But I expect Owain Glyndwr's mam was late back from the milk. They'll have had to wait for the pony.'

'Keep your eyes skinned for the Special Branch,' Gareth warned him.

'Special Branch? Here? You must be joking.' Not even Meredith's romantic vision could encompass that bizarre notion. 'Don't be daft. Surely they got more things on their plate than our demonstration? The whole bloody island's in revolt, man.'

Gareth shook his head sadly.

'I'm sorry, Mr Chairman. I have to say that you are naïve politically. Every expression of the people's desire for freedom, out they come. Photographing.' Gareth managed to make it sound like a pornographic exercise. 'Photographing. And taking names.'

For it must not be imagined that Gareth did not have visions of his own. The idea of a demonstration had come apparently as an afterthought at the last meeting of the Society of the Red Hand of Glyndwr. In fact the idea had been planted deliberately by Gareth who was feeling very left out in the freedom struggle.

The resolution to demonstrate had been carried unanimously, but there had been few volunteers to take part. Members were too anxious to watch the *Gêm*. And they were slightly nervous of the reaction of the contestants if there was any interruption of their ritual slaughter.

In the end Mrs Probert Milk's son, Danny Half-Pint, who was a 'natural', was prevailed upon to take the part of Owain Glyndwr. He had begged the loan of the pony his mother used on the milk round and Meredith had made him a suit of armour out of cardboard covered in kitchen foil. Lady teachers at Meredith's school had seemed the wisest choice for the body of the demonstration and as banner carriers. Whatever else they were, the *Gêm* fighters were chivalrous to a man. They would never hit a lady.

'Bound to be late,' muttered Gareth gloomily. What chance had an activist got? You can't make a revolution with a cardboard Owain Glyndwr and a rebel army of lady school teachers, he told himself. Catch Lenin crossing Germany to liberate Russia on a bloody pony he'd borrowed from his mother's milk float?

Across the beach Tim, too, was troubled.

'Meet Sir Huw? Are you quite sure this is the time or place?'

'What better, my boy?' said Sir Pelham, who had been eyeing Sir Huw's brandy flask and electric fire with longing. 'Social gathering and all that. Public show of good fellowship. Splendid. Excellent PR, I should have thought.'

'He may not want to shake hands, Sir Pelham. I believe he can be very difficult.'

'Rubbish, Crisp. Use your initiative. You've let this fellow brainwash you. You introduce me to the daughter and I'll get her to take me to her father. She won't refuse me because of you, and he won't snub me because of her. *Quod erat Demonstrandum*.'

The idea of the meeting was not appealing, but when he weighed Sir Pelham's pride against the prospect of talking to Ceri, Tim was surprised how her slight form weighed more heavily than Sir Pelham's massive bulk.

'If that is your wish, Permanent Secretary,' he said, and disappeared quickly into the crowd.

When he found her, Ceri was apprehensive.

'I'm not sure it's a good idea. My father's in a very strange mood. He's got something up his sleeve. I don't know what. But I fancy it's nothing your boss is going to enjoy.'

'Oh, come. Surely he wouldn't attempt anything against a representative of the Queen's ministers in broad daylight among all these people?'

Ceri rewarded him with a pitying look.

'You really don't know dad, do you?'

But she was finding it increasingly difficult to refuse anything to this handsome young man. In the free-for-all contest which was going on in her emotions, biology was ahead by two falls and a submission against common sense, which frequently loses in such contests.

'Very well,' she said. 'Come on. I'll introduce you and you can ask him yourself. But don't say I didn't warn you.'

If the meeting between Crisp and the man who had unknowingly been cast in the role of his father-in-law was only moderately successful, the one which followed with Sir Pelham was disastrous.

Of course, it might have been by accident that Grout chose to accelerate just at the moment Sir Pelham came within range of the exhaust. People who later claimed that they had heard Sir Huw give his driver the range and firing instructions could easily have been mistaken.

Whatever the truth, it is a fact that the moment Sir Pelham appeared at the edge of the crowd, Grout pumped his pedal and the Permanent Secretary disappeared in a cloud of acrid exhaust fumes. When it cleared away it had taken much of his dignity with it. Spluttering from a mixture of arrogance and asphyxia, his round pig-like eyes streaming, he completed the last yards of his journey with a huge red silk handkerchief clutched to his nose.

ap Coch was mortified.

'I'm frightfully sorry,' he apologised, while Sir Huw glared at him. 'Do come up in the Land Rover.'

Sir Pelham returned an unfriendly glare.

'Thank you, no,' he spluttered. 'I merely wished to speak briefly to Sir Huw. I was hoping we might arrange a formal meeting later today.'

Sir Huw's eyes glinted, a warning which Sir Pelham ignored as he pushed Crisp forward with a hissed, 'Introduce me, you fool.'

'May I present Sir Pelham Effyngham-Blynd?' said Tim. 'Sir Pelham is Permanent Secretary to the Secretary of State for Wales,' he went on lamely, since the name had no visible effect on ap Gryfydd.

'Baronet?' he barked, and had the satisfaction of seeing Sir Pelham flush.

'Alas, no. Hereditary titles were abandoned some years ago.'

'Oh, bloody life-renter,' muttered ap Gryfydd with barely concealed disgust. 'And what can I do for you?'

With commendable dignity Sir Pelham ignored the hostility, though he was nervously aware that it was spreading through the crowd. Somewhere he heard a woman muttering, 'Social Services, 'e is, mark my words. Only pretendin' to be an undertaker,' and he knew without looking that she had orange hair. Hurriedly he went on:

'I wouldn't wish to detain you now, Sir Huw. Perhaps we might meet later at your house?'

Once again the dangerous twinkle blazed in ap Gryfydd's eyes.

'Who knows, Sir Pelham?' he cooed. 'Who knows, indeed? Get a lot of visitors at Plas Becod,' he added darkly.

'Quite, quite. Perhaps I can get my assistant here to arrange a convenient time?'

ap Gryfydd smiled.

'My house is your home,' he said with a sweet innocence which brought a quizzical look from ap Coch. 'In the meantime, don't let me keep you from enjoying our humble little festival. No, indeed. I should stand over there on that hillock.' And he pointed to a superb vantage point which, strangely no one had occupied.

Not even the trained observers sent to report the scene for the *North Wales Chronicle* were able to give a coherent account of what followed when Sir Pelham took up his place on the hill. Even that short journey was not accomplished without a contretemps.

'You're wearin' the 'at,' a voice at his side hissed accusingly.

Startled, Sir Pelham stopped and looked round to find his acquaintance of the previous night had caught him by his coat tails.

'My good man,' he began.

'I'm not your good man. I'm The Fool, see? It's *my* hat gets burned.' And he pointed to his head where a battered homburg sat rather self-consciously. Incongruously it was draped in ribands of coloured paper. Though it bore only the vaguest structural similarity to the lovingly brushed homburg under which Sir Pelham was now pinking with rage, there was a family likeness.

'Man and boy I worn this 'at,' the Fool told him with pride. 'Laid out in his coffin with it, my da' was, till the moment the lid was nailed down. Given to me by the undertaker. Just before we left for the cemetery. "Wear it," he said. "You're the Fool now. No one can take it away." Not even London folks,' he added darkly. 'It's my 'at gets burned, see?'

'I'm very glad to hear it,' spluttered Sir Pelham, and tugging his coat tail free, he made for his place on the hill.

Glaring after him the Fool waited until Sir Pelham was safely out of range of even the most wayward match, then he took his place with becoming dignity on the Fool's Stone, a large boulder at the head of the beach. He raised his official headgear, and with a final withering glare at Sir Pelham's distant homburg, replaced it firmly on his head and addressed the crowd.

'Knows nothin' about inflammable 'ats,' he informed them. 'Burnin' 'ats is in its infancy in London,' he added. 'It's my 'at gets burned. Tradition, see? Stands to sense.'

A great roar of approval met this short speech, after which a man stepped forward with a burning taper and ceremonially lit the ribands which had been soaked in paraffin. In an instant the Hat was surrounded by a satisfactory blaze. As though to prove his right to his hereditary office, the Fool did not move it from his head until there was a slight singeing of the sparse hair he retained. Then, raising it slowly from his head, he waved it at the crowd.

'Now that,' he said with quiet satisfaction, 'is what *I* call an inflammable 'at.'

The raised hat was the signal for the *Gêm* to start, and not before time to judge from the roar which rose from the two waiting teams of burly young men and was taken up in a fearsome baying from the crowd.

A horrified Sir Pelham realised why the hillock on which he stood had been shunned by the spectators. What he had taken for crowds on either side of his hill were, in fact, the opposing teams. And when a hugely grinning Twdr Plas Drynkin scrambled up beside him the terrible truth dawned. For Twdr was carrying a long, battered leather cylinder which had the appearance of a young tree trunk. The hillock was in the centre of the game. At Sir Pelham's feet the teams growled and circled. In his fevered imagination they were transformed into ravening hounds, snapping and leaping at him, as, with arms stretched, the *Gêm*'s players jockeyed and jumped at the cylinder which Twdr swung above them like a massive bone.

There was no sign in him now of the staid treasurer of the District Council. The prosperous and dignified land-owner had vanished and in his stead was a capering tribesman, urging the teams into fury with a torrent of archaic Welsh taunts.

Despite the cold, Twdr was in his shirt sleeves and muscles swelled under the striped flannel until it seemed that the stitching must break. Sir Pelham watched him mesmerised. No longer a senior civil servant, he knew that he had become a ritual sacrifice. The 'hood' was swinging over his head now as Twdr whirled round and round. In the tiny corner of his mind that was still functioning Sir Pelham sensed that the 'hood' was coming nearer and nearer to his head with every revolution of Twdr's body. Inches from the luckless Whitehall man's head it suddenly soared and then dipped a fraction beyond his face. Finally, inevitably, it struck him a resounding thwack on the shoulder blades and precipitated him in a graceful parabola onto the stretched arms of the shouting men below.

'Better than a bloody five iron,' roared Sir Huw. 'If he could hit like that at the Golf he'd be Welsh champion.'

ap Coch stared at him in amazement.

'In God's name, what have you done now?' he gasped.

'Done? Hijacked the bugger. Look!' And he nodded his head towards the game where the Groeslon team, Sir Pelham held over their heads like a parcel, dashed for the edge of the crowd which parted before them.

Sir Pelham was beyond sensation. The squeals he emitted and the anguished kicking were purely instinctive. He hardly noticed when he was bundled into the back of a waiting van. He retained only a confused memory of a large, smoke-blackened face which appeared at the rear of the van seconds before its doors were closed. The owner of the face was carrying Sir Pelham's homburg which had fallen off on his passage to the van. The Fool tossed it in with a leer of triumph.

'And take your bloody 'at with you,' he said, flicking the still smouldering ribands of his own.

Neither hat escaped permanent damage that day but a third piece of headgear was damaged beyond repair. The stunned silence which followed the *Gêm* was broken by the sound of military music. Drunk on sensation, every head turned to the source, an extraordinary procession, which was making its way to the beach. From a loud-speaker tied to the roof of a second blue van the amplified sound of a record of 'Men of Harlech' was being thumped out by a Guards' band. And it was obviously unnerving an elderly pony upon which sat a figure in cardboard armour. Behind and around him marched, in uncertain step, a group of grimly Amazon lady schoolteachers carrying banners, only to scatter as the kidnappers' van bore down on them along the narrow road. Abandoning formation and hurling their banners away, the lady teachers leapt for safety. Most of the banners fell harmlessly to the ground. But one, thrown with more nervous vigour than the rest, struck Danny Half-Pint in the back of his cardboard armour, pushing him, even as he brandished his tin-plate sword, out of the saddle and into the road where he lay kicking on his back like a ruffled ladybird. Only the pony retained its composure. After a first questioning whinny it turned to look with compassion and contempt at its displaced rider; then it trotted quietly to the roadside where it began to graze in a marked manner.

The roar of laughter from the crowd drowned the cries of rage Gareth Jenkyn uttered as he dashed his worker's heath-mixture cap from his head, hurled it to the ground and proceeded to dance on its centre button.

'Bloody revolutionaries,' he raged, shaking his fists at Meredith. 'I've seen better revolutions on a gramophone turn-table. Standing here like a couple of pricks at a wedding while they snatch the biggest political prize from under our noses.'

They were joined by Danny Half-Pint, still wearing the tattered remnants of his armour. As he scrambled up the bank to join them he pushed up the visor of his still intact helmet. His anxious face peered out at them, apologetic and concerned.

'Sorry, we're a bit late then, Gareth,' he told his leader winningly. 'The old pony would keep stoppin' where mam delivers milk. Then we had to wait until the *North Wales Chronicle* took our picture.'

Meredith sadly surveyed the shuffling and embarrassed milk boy.

'Never mind,' he told him. 'Look grand in the paper on Thursday.'

Across the dunes yet another acrimonious conversation was taking place. Sadly the participants in this were Ceri and her admirer Tim Crisp. Both those spirited youngsters were hopping mad.

Tim was furious.

'It's the most appalling piece of juvenile hooliganism I've ever witnessed,' he said. 'Do you realise what's going to happen now? I'll tell you. Your father and every one of these elderly juvenile delinquents is going to spend the next ten years working his way through a mountain of porridge. God, I enjoy a joke, but this is sheer stupidity.

I don't know how you could let yourself be a party to it.'

Ceri was astounded.

'A party? Don't be totally cretinous. You surely don't think I knew what was going to happen, do you? And don't forget, I warned you. I told you it was madness to bring that pompous ass to the *Gêm*. But would you listen? Oh, no! You knew best. And now when your stupidity has got you in a mess all you can think of doing is to blame me!'

She glared at him. Then with a toss of her raven hair and a contemptuous 'Men!' she stormed off.

'And don't forget, we want him back,' Tim shouted after her.

That evening in a room in the Eagle Tower of Plas Becod Sir Pelham, bruised and subdued, looked about him gloomily. There was no window in the circular stone room, only an arrow slit through which he caught occasional glimpses of a wild, storm-tossed Celtic Sea. There was no door to the room, nothing more than a trap-door in the floor. But it was a comfortable enough billet. He sat in a wing armchair, sheltered from the draught from the arrow slit, before a roaring log fire. His clothes, which had been brought from the Groeslon, hung in a press. There was a curtained bed at the far side of the fire, a jug and ewer stood on an ancient sideboard and on a small table at his side was a decanter of wine and a glass, a cold grouse, fruit and cheese. In an alcove off the main room was a primitive garderobe with a chute which fell to the sea. There were books and magazines, even a portable radio. In other circumstances Sir Pelham might have enjoyed his richly medieval surroundings but he was still seething from his interview earlier in the evening with a triumphant, though courteously hospitable, Sir Huw. Sir Pelham had been very much the outraged Mandarin.

'Are you aware,' he demanded, 'that you have kidnapped the representative of Her Britannic Majesty's Government and that the repercussions are likely to be extremely grave?'

'I expect they'll send a gun-boat for you,' Sir Huw replied drily.

'You don't appear to be taking this very seriously. I can assure you that I am.'

'Well, you're the one that's locked up, so I suppose that's natural. But you did say you wanted to come and see me. And here you are. Safe and snug.'

'Safe and snug? Locked up in a stone tower with a gale howling round my ears?'

'Come, hardly a gale, surely?' Sir Huw crossed to the window slit. 'Stiffish breeze. Nothing more. Do you the power of good.'

'And how long do you propose keeping me?'

'Oh, not long. Just till your Prime Minister agrees to meet me and discuss Tad's independence.'

'Tad's independence?' Sir Pelham was scornful. 'You surely don't imagine there's the slightest chance of *that*?'

'In that case you're going to be here a very long time. So I should get some sleep as soon as you've had your supper.

And with that Sir Huw lifted the trap-door and stepped onto the stairs below.

'Wait!' Sir Pelham cried. 'Don't go yet. This meeting. What did you have in mind?'

'Remember Rhodesia?' asked Sir Huw. Sir Pelham shuddered. 'One of my people was telling me that when Wilson met Smith they didn't trust each other enough to meet either in London or Salisbury. Right?'

Sir Pelham nodded weakly.

'Met on a destroyer, I believe? Name of the *Tiger*?'

Sir Pelham nodded again.

'Well, we don't have a destroyer, of course. But we've got a nice ferry, *Queen of Tad*. I thought we might meet on that.'

'On a ferry boat? Out of the question.'

'On the contrary. Train from Euston to Bangor. Brisk little row out to the *Queen* and I'll be waiting to pipe the PM aboard.'

'Unthinkable. The Cabinet will never agree.'

'It never does,' rejoined ap Gryfydd, and bolting the trap-door behind him, he descended the stairs below, chuckling happily.

CHAPTER SIXTEEN

'Out of the question,' said the Prime Minister some months later. 'The Cabinet will never agree.'

The Cabinet Secretary shook his head and the PM quivered with alarm.

'D'you think they will?'

The Cabinet Secretary nodded his head firmly.

'No alternative, I'm afraid, Prime Minister. I've sounded them out and I must tell you that the majority view is that it is time for An Initiative. They know how strongly you feel about initiatives.'

'Yes, but not *my* initiative, Sir Peregrine. I initiate for others. Clambering about in rowing boats hardly accords with the dignity of the Queen's First Minister.'

'Harold did it.'

'Harold would do anything to get his picture in the papers. Surely there's some other way? Can't we just give them the damned island?'

'Alas, no. We were, as you know, in process of setting up a steering committee to investigate just such a course of action. Then there was that dreadful business in the High Court.'

The Prime Minister groaned.

'How on earth *that* decision was reached I'll never know. Imagine a High Court judge agreeing that the issue of UDI should go to the International Court.'

'It was a Welsh judge, of course. And a Welsh jury.'

'That's another thing. What about jury vettings? Couldn't we have got some English jurists?'

The Attorney General, who was also present at the Downing Street meeting, sighed.

'In Caernarfon, Prime Minister?'

'Then why was it held in Caernarfon?'

'Precedent,' the Attorney General explained. 'Cases are normally heard in the nearest Crown Court for the convenience of witnesses. And Canter, who appeared for Sir

Huw, argued some precedent from the eighteenth century.'

'That old fool,' the PM snorted.

'It certainly made an impression on the jury when a retired judge appeared for the plaintiffs. He's a very well respected figure in that part of the world. Truth to tell, I think his Brother on the bench was inclined to listen sympathetically to a fellow judge whatever he said.'

'Brother?'

'Only in the legal sense. In fact it is my understanding they are only second cousins.'

'The same family?'

'In that part of the world the entire Circuit is related. And most of the jurymen, too, I fear. It makes for very long hearings. It's the refreshers, you know. Some of the divorce hearings last almost as long as the marriages.'

'And has it any chance of succeeding at the UN?' the PM wanted to know.

'Every chance, I regret to say,' the Attorney General replied. 'I gather from our man there that the entire Third World will support the application for the issue to be judged at the Hague. They are naturally very sensitive about Home Rule. And that, of course, means the Iron Curtain countries will back it too.'

'But, surely, it will be thrown out by the International Court?' The PM was pleading now.

'It's by no means certain. It all hinges on the charter, d'you see? When that Blair woman was called as an expert witness she was able to prove the age of the paper on which the charter was written. And then a graphologist identified twenty-four points of similarity between the handwriting on the charter and that on a document supplied by the Public Records Office which was of Henry VII's undoubted authorship . . .'

'Another damned Welshman.'

'Yes, but a *prima facie* case was established. And as Canter ably pointed out, not only ap Gryfydd and his family, but the entire Gorsedd have amply fulfilled the charter's military requirements in every war since Bosworth Field.'

The PM groaned.

'But if they're going to win anyway, what's the point in going on this frightful boat?'

The Secretary of the Cabinet came as near bridling as his distinguished office permitted him.

'There is the question of Effyngham-Blynd.'

The PM replied with an expletive that might have been an attempt to repeat the name. Sir Peregrine blushed and continued.

'He has been in captivity for six months, Prime Minister . . .'

'Captivity? Secret Intelligence tells me he's joined some damned yachting club. And he's living the life of Riley in a cliff-top villa. Even, so I'm told, taken up with that archivist woman.'

Early in the Tad campaign Secret Intelligence had succeeded in planting an agent on the Island. In the way of Welsh rural communities his cover had been blown within a fortnight. But he had been an agreeable enough young man, and as Will Looms Lloyd George, with whom he was lodging posing as a newspaper reporter, pointed out, 'Everyone's got a livin' to earn.' So beyond calling him – behind his back, of course – 'Jones the Spy', in memory of an old Welsh joke, he had been allowed to follow his calling.

The revelation in the early 'eighties that Cambridge University had provided a series of Soviet moles in MI5 and MI6 had made Sir Huw snort. Ever since he had been unable to take the Secret Services seriously. 'Jesus College, Magdalen College,' he told ap Coch. 'I suppose they'll have to call the next college Judas Iscariot!'

Jones the Spy had reported that a fortnight after Sir Pelham had been hijacked, partly due to the insistence of Ceri but mostly because his company was irritating, ap Gryfydd had moved him into a holiday cottage near the Moorings. In return for his parole ap Coch had put Sir Pelham up for membership of the Club. Tim had stayed on the island, too. Partly out of loyalty, but mostly in order to repair the rift between himself and Ceri. As to Miss Magersfontein-Blair, her sister's home baking – it was said on the island that her fancy cakes were so light they had to be nailed to the table to prevent them floating to the ceiling – and her own infinite capacity as an audience had quite won Sir Pelham's old heart. He had become, as a result, a much nicer person, as many another had under the potent magic of the island. Often Jones the Spy made up a fourth at bridge in the sister's pretty cottage. It was an admirable arrangement all round. He was able to collect the gossip from both sides and Tim was able to get away for evening walks on the shore with Ceri.

None of these happy arrangements, alas, weighed with the Prime Minister.

'Can't we snatch him?'

Sir Peregrine coughed with embarrassment.

'I'm afraid he won't come. Claims he's given his parole.' Privately he had learned from Jones the Spy that the four had entered the island's Bridge Tournament and Sir Huw and partner had every chance of winning. But he saw no reason to pass on that particular piece of intelligence. 'And, of course, he *is* the only representative of central government. Our only line, in fact, to the rebels.'

'And I suppose I'm really going in order to yank him out like some political 007?'

'Indeed, no, Prime Minister,' the Attorney General broke in. 'Much more serious issues are at stake. It is felt among senior members of your Cabinet that it would be a mistake to let this issue be thrashed out in the full glare of the public arena. The publicity would be enormous and politically very damaging. We must, at all costs, pre-empt the matter reaching the International Court. There are the by-elections coming up.'

This, he knew, was always an effective goad to the most recalcitrant of prime ministers. As always, it worked.

'Very well. What must I do?'

'As we see it, there is only one thing you can do. Offer the island Dominion Status.' Seeing the Prime Minister's look of incredulity he hurried on. 'There is the precedent of the Isle of Man. The island would still be part of the British Isles but, in theory, not of the UK. That would create an illusion of liberty but we would still retain some hold on the purse strings.'

'Is that important?'

'Indeed it is. Once the island has a measure of independence it will attract a great deal of investment. Already the leap in its income is quite staggering. If we merely established a "Common Purse", as was done with the Isle of Man, it would give us five per cent of Tad's national Treasury. In the Isle of Man the Common Purse only covers the national income from customs and excise dues. Your colleagues in the Cabinet would argue for a larger sum, say twenty per cent, and they would wish it to be based not on national revenue but on the GNP.'

'Even so, it can hardly be a staggering sum.'

'On the contrary. In 1969 the Isle of Man had only one merchant bank, yet within five years deposits in the banking sector totalled two hundred million pounds. Goodness knows what they are now. I'm still awaiting my brief from the Treasury and you know how they hate talking about money.

'The point is,' he continued, 'we are in the identical position with Tad that the British Government was in vis-à-vis the Isle of Man in the eighteenth century. Then HMG's priority was to stop the smuggling. With quite criminal myopia the island was allowed to get away with murder in return for UK customs control. Our priorities now are different. There's an awful lot of money floating round the world and HMG must try to get a share of it. Operating, as it does at the moment, on an ad hoc basis, money is nevertheless pouring into Tad at a staggering rate. Their revenue from the oil company alone must be phenomenal, not to mention the landing tax on tourists. It's a fiver a head but who begrudges that when cigarettes are only twenty pence for twenty? And this year they will be having their first crops of home-grown tobacco. When they have a commercial tobacco industry they will be able practically to give the stuff away.'

Sir Peregrine broke in.

'A chum in customs and excise was telling me that people in Bangor are finding it cheaper to do their weekly shopping on the island even with the tourist tax. And the smuggling industry on the North Wales coast is at its highest level in recorded history. They distil their own spirits now, d'you see? And damned fine stuff it is. By another of those lucky coincidences they seem to attract, the island water is quite indistinguishable from the water in the Highlands of Scotland. They're making the most lovely single malts. One called Tad's Delight is particularly fine . . . or so I believe,' he added lamely, noticing the PM's glare.

'But, surely,' the Prime Minister pointed out, 'they must realise they are in the pound seats? Why should they agree to Dominion Status when they can go to the International Court – did you know, by the way, that damned judge granted them legal aid?' The others nodded miserably. 'Go to the International Court, I repeat, and walk out free of any links with the UK at all?'

'That's quite true,' said the Attorney General. 'But, if I may say so, I don't believe that they really want to leave the UK at all.'

'Difficult to swallow that one. Everyone wants to leave the UK, surely?'

'With respect, no. Look at ap Gryfydd. He believes in tradition. When you boil down his complaints they're quite trivial. I don't believe he'd ever have thought of UDI if it hadn't been for that damned nonsense from the Post Office. He and his confounded Gorsedd are all old men with very full private lives. Already they must be finding that government is a full time job. Can you imagine what it would be like when they've got total responsibility? It's my belief that if we offer them Dominion Status they will jump at it.'

There was silence in the Cabinet Room for several minutes. Finally the Prime Minister's mind was made up.

'Very well, I'll go. Oh, why did I allow you to persuade me to sell our last destroyer to Rod Stewart as a retirement home? We might at least have put on something of a show. Have you any further advice?'

The tone was not encouraging but the Attorney General was sufficiently sure of his victory to fire a last mocking salvo.

'Well, I should certainly take your sheepskin, Prime Minister. I understand the wind in the straits can be quite bracing.'

The meeting was just on the point of breaking up in a mood of mutual ill will when Sir Peregrine made the noisy gear change in his throat which indicated he had something else to say.

'Yes?' The Prime Minister's tone was brusque.

'About Sir Pelham.'

'D'you want me to take a sheepskin for him?'

'Oh, certainly not. Heaven forfend. But I do feel that his return to freedom must form part of your agenda.'

'Frankly, I don't care if I never see him again.'

'I understand, Prime Minister, but, frankly, it's the look of the thing. His – ahem – incarceration has had a very marked effect on other senior civil servants in his grade. I had the greatest difficulty last week in setting up a Commission of Inquiry into that business of the motorway at Barnsley.'

'Difficulty?'

'Yes, Attorney General. There was a distinct frisson in the Service. After all, the idea of being hijacked and held in durance vile in Barnsley is not at all attractive. The only man in the appropriate grade I could persuade to chair the commission would do so only on the assurance that he would be escorted by two members of the Special Branch.'

'*Two?*'

'Yes, I fear the Special Branch operatives are equally reticent about leaving the metropolis on their own.'

The Prime Minister froze him with a look that was positively glacial, and only partially thawed by the frosty smile which followed.

'I've got a splendid idea.' The cold eyes lit with malice. 'I'll put his name before the Sovereign.'

'How kind,' murmured Sir Peregrine. 'An honour I feel will much compensate him for the rigours of his captivity.'

'An honour indeed. He shall be the first Governor General of Tad.'

Sir Peregrine was horrified.

'Oh, no, Prime Minister.'

'Oh, yes, Cabinet Secretary. It will give him the opportunity to improve his bridge game.'

CHAPTER SEVENTEEN

The *Queen of Tad* had seen better days, but they had been so long ago her creaky, tar-soaked timbers held no memory of them.

Half a century earlier on the beaches of Dunkirk only the bravest soldiers could be persuaded to board her. She had been old even then and many preferred the prison camp to crossing the choppy Channel in a paddle-steamer they feared had been chartered from a low budget musical comedy.

She had a single central funnel which resembled an extended index finger and a small, round body which so resembled a clenched fist that at sea she seemed to be pointing, a pessimistic direction sign, at heaven as her mariners' destination. She looked not so much designed as drawn by an imaginative cartoon animator. More anthropomorphic than aquatic, there was about her an unmistakable air of early Walt Disney.

She steams into our story at the end of a passage from Tad across Cardigan Bay, past Belan Fort and through the tricky channel of the Menai Straits. As she approached Penrhyn Pier she wheezed rather than whistled the news of her arrival, and sighed gratefully when mooring ropes fell with a wet clatter on her decks and she felt herself being pulled to her berth.

The PM's two elegant and willowy secretaries were thunderstruck.

'One assumes,' observed one, 'that we will go aboard two by two?'

Her companion's eyes, however, were fixed on a villainous pot-shelf of faces which peered down at them over the rail of the bridge. One more lecherous than the rest was mentally undressing the two secretaries in a forgetful, half instinctive way. Morgan Organ, the ferry steward whose nickname owed nothing to music, never missed an opportunity.

'And which one do you suppose is Noah?' the first secretary went on as she followed her friend's gaze.

'I don't know, but if that one doesn't get his hot little eyes out of my panties I'm going straight back on the next train.'

It was obvious to Morgan that he was being talked about. There was no doubt he had made a conquest. He raised a greasy, denim cap that had burrowed into a mass of hair which seemed to be unadulterated Castrol and leered.

The second secretary shuddered. 'And which one do you think is Noah?' she repeated, mesmerised.

'Who can tell? They all appear to be drunk. And who can blame them. I wouldn't cross a damp field, let alone Cardigan Bay, in that boat.'

'Thank God we don't have to,' the second secretary said. 'The PM has refused point blank to go in a rowing boat. The meeting is to be held in dock. I suppose they are tying those ropes to her to prevent her sinking at her moorings.'

A convoy of ministerial limousines, led by the PM's Toyota, swept down the quay.

'They're here,' the second secretary said. 'I wonder what the PM's reaction is going to be.'

The Prime Minister's initial reaction was a point blank refusal to get out of the car.

'But, Prime Minister, I have Sir Huw's assurance that the ferry will not leave the quay,' the Secretary of State urged.

'That's not the point.' Icily. 'I doubt very much whether that tub *could* leave the quay. My question is whether she can remain above the surface even in that position.'

The towering Old Testament figure of Sir Huw appeared at the top of the gang plank. He was wearing oilskins.

'He looks as though he's stepped straight off a cod-liver oil label.'

'That is Sir Huw, Prime Minister.'

A second figure appeared at his side. Incongruously he was wearing a bowler hat and carrying a tightly furled umbrella.

'And I suppose that's his keeper.'

'Colonel ap Coch, actually. And I suppose, in a manner of speaking, he is.'

'And very welcome to him he is. Well, come along,' getting reluctantly out of the car, 'let's get it over with.'

As the ministerial party walked down the quay Sir Huw

muttered an instruction to Colonel ap Coch, then went below to the cramped saloon where the 'summit' was to be held. ap Coch picked his elegant way down the gang plank, and unfurling his umbrella with a flourish, held it over the party and escorted them aboard.

The PM looked with disfavour round the tiny saloon, then walked firmly over to the formica-topped table at which Sir Huw was waiting. He rose in greeting.

Instant affability touched the PM's face.

'Sir Huw, a great pleasure.'

'Good morning,' said Sir Huw, and sat down.

A square of card, curling at the edges, lay on the table top.

'The agenda, I presume?'

'The menu, actually,' replied Sir Huw. 'Do you fancy anything?'

The PM shuddered. 'Perhaps not quite yet. Shall we get down to business? A pleasure afterwards.' Another imperceptible shudder.

The opening skirmishes were short.

'Distinguished military career . . . sorry that we should have to meet in these distressing circumstances. Departmental misunderstandings. Unfortunate. What must be done to restore the status quo?' from the Prime Minister. And from Sir Huw a passionate diatribe about bureaucracy and private rights.

At the next table, studiously ignoring each other, ap Coch and the Secretary of State for Wales sat like seconds at a prize fight straining to hear what their principals were saying.

The Prime Minister got in the first flurry of blows. 'Illegal action. Possibility of criminal proceedings. Occupation of Tad one of the avenues explored by HMG.'

But Sir Huw parried easily. A practised and wily negotiator, it soon became obvious to the PM that Sir Huw had a hidden ammunition. Certainly the threats weren't working. Shift of footwork. A feint.

'Prepared to open discussions, the interest of national unity, on a return to county status . . .' contemptuously parried. Guard dropped. Inviting opening. 'As a final concession and in the light of the interim court hearings HMG prepared to offer Tad Dominion Status. Valuable concessions. Parity with the Isle of Man. Inestimable benefits. Autonomy . . .' the PM's voice trailed off, but the brain was busy. Damn the man, he's smiling. He knows something. He's waiting for something. What's happening?

A flurry among the officials at the door. The PM watched, controlling a mounting anxiety, as one of the Number 10 staff pushed through the group carrying a thin file of paper which he handed to the Secretary of State. The PM saw the minister start. Oh God, the thought came, don't let it be another by-election. The minister was signalling. An adjournment, that's it. Play for time.

'The proposals are far reaching, I realise.' Smooth, imperturbable. Not a trace of anxiety in the voice as the PM rose. 'Perhaps a short adjournment while you confer with your colleague?'

'No, don't you go, Prime Minister,' Sir Huw also rose, cooing. 'ap Coch and I will wait outside. We've dressed for it. I think your people have got something they want to tell you.'

Oilskins creaking, Sir Huw signalled to ap Coch and the two men stepped out onto the deck. They were both smiling broadly.

Inside the saloon the Prime Minister sat stricken. Staring at a sheet of flimsy paper in the open file on the table. It was a decoded transcription of a long coded cable which lay at its side.

'They can't . . .'

'I'm very much afraid,' the Secretary of State supplied, 'they already have. Less than an hour ago, according to the cable. The nine judges met in chambers at the International Court and . . .'

But he had lost the Prime Minister who was reading the judgment precis from the cable.

'The authenticity of the charter has been established beyond doubt by the national court,' it read. 'Our task is merely to establish whether the appellant and his family have fulfilled the conditions under which the contract was made.' More preamble, and then: 'The court has been impressed by the distinguished service, which, as is evident from military records placed before it, the appellant gave to his country during World War II. Further historical evidence submitted clearly establishes that members of his family have fought for the British Crown during every major engagement since, and including, Bosworth Field. Indeed, there is evidence of ap Gryfydds on the knights' rolls of Crecy, Poitiers and Agincourt. There can be no question but that the contract has been amply fulfilled. It is therefore the judgment of this court that the appellant's claim to sovereignty of the island of Tad is amply proved. And we do so find.'

Outside the saloon, in the drizzling rain, among the odour of fish boxes and wrapped in disreputable oilskins, King Huw I of Tad and Becod was musing gently.

'Nice of old Canter to ring us from the court,' he said.

'Very,' ap Coch agreed. 'Wonder how they are taking it in there?' and he jerked his head at the saloon.

'Badly, if I'm any judge,' ap Gryfydd grinned.

After a lengthy interval a confused aide appeared in the doorway of the saloon and coughed discreetly.

'Gentlemen, if you don't mind? The Prime Minister is quite ready for you now.'

Lesser mortals might have displayed chagrin about the loss of two islands, a voting population of two thousand and the prospect of an injection of large sums of capital. But the Prime Minister was made of sterner stuff.

'May I congratulate you, sir!' That consummate politician greeted ap Gryfydd. 'To my mind the very best possible decision. A veritable judgment of Solomon. Perhaps you will permit me, on behalf of HMG, to be the first to congratulate you on what I will, nay must, describe as the redressing of an Ancient Wrong.'

'Do tell the Queen and the Prince of Wales there was nothing personal,' ap Gryfydd broke in, to a firm, 'Hear, hear' from ap Coch.

'Please,' the PM raised an admonitory hand, 'please believe me that no one would entertain such a thought. It is my firm understanding that all of my ministers and officials who have had any dealings with you at all here are, to a man, united in their approval of the statesmanlike nature of your good self and your – ahem – Cabinet.' It was plain that the last word had cost the PM a great deal. 'Yes. United. And I am sure, nay positive, that you will bring those great qualities to bear in the delicate negotiations between our two, our two – ahem – countries.'

'Delicate negotiations?' ap Gryfydd echoed.

'To be sure. To be sure.' The Prime Minister rubbed practised hands together. 'There must be treaties. Yes, indeed. And aid. As an emergent country you will need aid, of course.'

Thank you, we don't need any money,' ap Gryfydd said. 'We're doing quite well as a matter of fact. Things all right with you?'

'Ha. Ha.' The laugh was hollow. A noble try, but those who heard it detected the faint rustle of envy. 'Ha. Ha. Capital jest. Yes, indeed. Perhaps you . . . perhaps *you* might lend *us* something, then? Ha. Ha.

'Good. Good.' The PM looked round the saloon. 'Well, that appears to cover the agenda for today. Very useful exchange of views. Most interesting. Bold, challenging ideas. Just what the world needs.'

'I haven't put forward any,' ap Gryfydd pointed out.

'Eh? No, no, of course not. Far too early for the small print. Broader issues first. Very good.' And then impatiently to the Cabinet Secretary: 'What is it, man?'

The Cabinet Secretary had been hopping from one foot to the other in agitation and semaphoring with his considerable eyebrows. Now he spoke urgently.

'Sir Pelham. Can we have Sir Pelham back?'

For a moment a look of animal savagery appeared on the PM's face. But it was quickly routed by a bland smile and lingered on only in the eyes.

'Sir Pelham? Ah, yes, to be sure, Sir Pelham.'

A brief pause to savour a tiny, vengeful thrust.

'I was wondering, Sir Huw . . .'

'Yes?'

'I believe you are acquainted with Sir Pelham Effyngham-Blynd?'

'We've met. He was a house guest for a while.'

'Quite, and most hospitable of you. The ancient tradition of the Celt, of course. I had an aunt in Rhyl. We were evacuated there in the war. And I have always thought of myself spiritually as Welsh.'

'Very kind. I'm sure we're greatly honoured.'

But the PM was proof against irony. That mighty brain was incapable of identifying it. The noble head merely nodded in recognition of a compliment.

'About Sir Pelham. I have the strongest feeling that it would be a crime to waste his unique knowledge of your island ways. And, indeed, less than just not to note, in some practical way, his role in the negotiations which had led to this – ah – happy conclusion. I therefore – subject, of course, to your approval – propose to recommend him to the Sovereign . . .' – a pause and a swift assassin's glance at the Cabinet Secretary – '. . . as Her Majesty's Consul to Tad.'

ap Gryfydd smiled and smoothed his whiskers. Then he remembered Ceri and the growing attachment he had seen over the past months.

'And his aide, Crisp? Make a very good First Secretary.'

'He's all yours,' said the Prime Minister with a seraphic smile. 'And now I bid you Good Day.'

CHAPTER EIGHTEEN

Tad's golden age began in brilliant sunshine. That year West Wales enjoyed the best summer since records were first kept. Even the farmers were happy. It rained at night and every morning sparkled like burnished steel.

It was the best summer for visitors too. The constant coverage in the press and on radio and TV had put the thought of a holiday on duty-free Tad in the minds of thousands of mainlanders. From overseas, too, the holiday-makers flocked. Some were disappointed the Gorsedd had laid down a maximum number of visitors and when that was reached no more bookings were accepted. But so keen was the world to see the tiny island that had won its freedom that they booked in at hotels and guest houses all along the mainland coast. Business boomed. Every front room on the island was transformed into a tea-room, a pottery or a souvenir shop. Facsimile copies of Tad's Charter, published under licence by a company which Sir Pelham had formed with Miss Blair, changed hands like hot bread.

Dr Margaret Wood, a lady geologist who lived on the island was co-opted onto the Gorsedd to advise on the exploitation of natural minerals. She drew up a scheme for pumping out the flooded workings of the undersea coal seams and the galleries in Mount Copr. No sooner had this been undertaken, with money supplied by the petrol company which had built the island's submerged pipeline, than the price of world copper went up by a penny a ton.

Overnight ap Gryfydd found himself a wealthy man and there were jobs galore for islanders working the coal and the copper.

Oddly, ap Gryfydd was gloomy. And it was a gloom which deepened with every balance sheet from his mining interests and every optimistic report from his holdings in a holiday complex which had grown out of disused warehouses on the jetty of Byndrynkin. As the islanders revelled in the new wealth that full employment brought and as money poured into the Tad coffers from the tourist tax, the shilling in the pound income tax, the oil company levy and the thousand and one new sources which Twdr Plas Drynkin and his adviser Tom Fort established, so Sir Huw became more and more withdrawn. ap Coch began to worry about him and one night over dinner with his old chieftain and Tom Fort he broached the question.

'Unhappy?' Sir Huw growled. 'Wouldn't you be?'

'But, ap Gryfydd, the money is pouring into the island treasury. Goodness knows what Plas Drynkin's windfall levy on the off-shore banking interests is going to bring in. You did buy shares, as I advised?'

'Oh, yes,' said ap Gryfydd bitterly. 'Bought them with the profits the mining company brought in.'

'Well then, you must be getting on to being a millionaire.'

'More than getting on,' ap Gryfydd sighed. 'I *am* a millionaire.'

'Well then,' said Fort, 'there you are then.'

'Where?'

'I'm sorry?'

'Where am I? I'll tell you where I am, I'm sitting on top of a pile of money I don't want, can't count. And I don't at all wish to buy the sort of things you're supposed to spend that kind of money on.'

'A lot of people would envy you.'

'And that's another thing. They do. I tell you, this island's changing. I can feel resentment. Resentment on Tad. I ask you! And what's more it's being stirred up by sewers like that Gareth Jenkyn.'

The news that Tad had become a sovereign kingdom had, strangely, been welcomed by Jenkyn. Although in his dreams he had seen himself as the British Lenin leading a revolution of the workers, a little voice had whispered that he really wasn't up to a job of that size. The United Kingdom was out of Jenkyn's league. Tad was different. Tad was small and still uncertain. Abandoning 'Glyndwr' without a trace of remorse, the next day he had founded the Tad's People's Party. Though its membership was small it was highly vocal and the newspaper it published was eagerly bought. True, the customers were mostly holiday-makers anxious for any off-beat souvenir of their stay on the unique island. But in almost every issue ap Gryfydd was attacked as a roaring capitalist exploiting the islanders in order to amass a great fortune.

'Oh, I shouldn't take any notice of his rantings,' argued Fort. 'Look what you've done. Full employment, the best schools and hospitals in Britain. We've doubled the old-age pension; any youngster who wants to go to university gets three times the UK grant; our fishing fleet is the most modern in Europe; there's not a house on the island that isn't a little palace.'

'But he's right, you see,' ap Gryfydd interrupted. 'I am amassing a fortune. Where he's wrong is in thinking I want one. Can't he realise I don't want to be a millionaire?'

'Give it away, then,' Fort offered unsympathetically.

'No use. Oh, I've thought of it. But there's no equable way of doing it. How do you work out who gets it? And when they get it what are they going to do with it? For it will change them. You know the old saying "You can tell what God thinks about money by the sort of people he gives it to"?'

Both men were silent now, wrapped in gloomy speculation. Only ap Coch was smiling.

'What a pity it is,' he said, 'what a pity that neither of you had the advantage of a musical education otherwise you could have solved the problem months ago.'

'How?'

'Gilbert and Sullivan.'

'Who?'

'Gilbert and Sullivan.'

'I don't think I know the firm,' Fort began. 'Oh, the opera chaps. D'Oyly Carte and all that.'

'Precisely,' ap Coch smiled reflectively. 'Wonderful operas. Seen 'em all. Gilbert and Sullivan and supper at the Cri.'

ap Gryfydd snarled.

'Only been once. Some damn great ox of a woman

supposed to be dying of consumption and a chap with dyed hair complaining about her tiny hand being frozen. Tiny hand! Fingers like saveloys! Dammit, ap Coch, this is supposed to be a serious discussion. You'll be tellin' us about ballet next.'

'You don't like ballet either, ap Gryfydd?' This from Fort.

'Like it? I should hope not. Damn pouf's football. Can't we please stick to the subject in hand? What am I goin' to do with all this blasted money? Finance Tad Opera Company? Overrun the island with sopranos? I am afraid I don't think much of that for an idea.'

ap Coch sighed.

'If I could only persuade you to listen for a moment to what I'm trying to tell you.'

'I'm financing no opera companies,' ap Gryfydd insisted. 'Caterwauling. All bosom and basso profundos!'

ap Coch waited patiently for his chief to finish.

'The fact is,' he said as ap Gryfydd subsided into intermittent snorts, 'the fact is I got rather hooked on G and S.'

'G and T more like,' snorted ap Gryfydd, but ap Coch ignored him.

'So much so that I bought a book of the lyrics of all the operas,' he continued. 'Dashed witty. Over the years it's become my favourite bedside reading. John Buchan apart, of course.'

'Read in bed?' ap Gryfydd was incredulous. 'How on earth d'ye manage to keep awake?'

'Largely by not having a decanter of port to my own cheek after supper. Anyway, this book doesn't just have their popular operas. It also has the ones that didn't quite make it. Including one of the last ones they wrote. It's an odd little piece. All about a self-governing island. It's called *Utopia Limited*.

'Very witty,' interrupted ap Gryfydd drily. 'Really, ap Coch . . .'

'If I might just speak? The opera is called *Utopia Limited* or *The Flowers of Progress*. It's about a tropical island where every want is supplied by a kindly monarch; where the islanders have no need to think because all their wants are anticipated and their opinions formed by the same kindly monarch.'

Here he looked at ap Gryfydd who stirred uneasily.

'He is assisted by two Wise Men.'

A 'hmph' from ap Gryfydd. He looked meaningfully at ap Coch, who, to his astonishment, burst into song.

'Oh make way for the Wise Men:
They are the prize men
Double-first in the
  World's University.
For though lovely this island
  (which is MY LAND)
They're the pride of UTOPIA
Cornucopia
is each in his mental fertility.
And they never make a blunder
And no wonder
For they're triumphs of infallibility . . .'

'Good God,' muttered ap Gryfydd.

'Anyway, the king decided to model his island on Great Britain.'

'Obviously mad,' observed ap Gryfydd, and then impatiently: 'What the devil has this to do with me?'

Clearly ap Coch was not to be allowed to reveal the plot of the opera. With a sigh he came to the point.

'Well, one of the characters who has been brought in to anglicise the island is a company promoter called Mr Goldbury. Rather a catching little tune he has . . .' and once more ap Coch burst into song.

'Stupendous loans to foreign thrones
I've largely advocated.
In ginger pops and peppermint
  drops I've largely speculated.
Their mines of gold . . .'

Catching ap Gryfydd's warning glare the song trailed off.

'Well, anyway, he advances the view that ruling Utopia is

too big for one small head. And he suggests turning the island into a Limited Company.'

Fort broke in now.

'Am I to understand that you want Tad to be governed on the joint stock principle? You're being very provoking tonight, ap Coch. What are you grinning at now?'

'Oddly,' replied ap Coch, 'that's more or less what the king says to Mr Goldbury. And I think you should follow the king's example when he sings,

'We'll go down to Posterity renowned
As the First Sovereign in Christendom
Who registered his Crown and Country under
The Joint Stock Company's
Act of sixty two.'

ap Gryfydd leaned forward.

'Are you serious?'

'Perfectly. Look here, ap Gryfydd, I've known you all your life. You really don't need money to enjoy yourself. A day with your hounds, a bit of fishing. Out on the tractor for the spring ploughing. Good God, you're still drinking that disgusting Home Brew while your fortune mounts like a snowdrift.

'Why not form a Limited Company of all the resources of the island with yourself as Chairman and the Gorsedd as the Board of Directors. They're all sensible men of enormous integrity. You can hand over the copper and the coal mines and such a sum as you may wish to capitalise it. Then you can issue shares equally among all the islanders. In that way they will be getting the benefit from the work they put in.'

'Yes, that's all very well, but what would I have to do as chairman? Sounds pretty time consuming.'

It was Fort's turn to laugh.

'Very little. When I was chairman of our company I spent two years designing my rose garden here on Tad.'

ap Gryfydd turned to him.

'Is this practicable?'

Fort shrugged.

'Perfectly. Wouldn't work in somewhere the size of the

UK, of course. But here on Tad. You really are becoming enormously wealthy, you know. And the population is quite small.'

'Sounds like Bolshevism,' growled ap Gryfydd.

'Certainly the Limited Company has all the benefits of Bolshevism. Only difference is that it works. And I do see what you mean about giving people money. Doesn't really help 'em very much. Either they don't know what to do with it and it worries them to death, or they go wild pissing it against a pub wall. Or they become miserly. Whichever way, it changes them for the worse. But in this way you wouldn't be giving them money, even in the form of shares. They'd be buying them off you with their skill and industry.'

'Yes,' insisted ap Gryfydd, 'but is it practical?'

'Perfectly,' Fort assured him. 'Need some working out. If I were you I'd keep control of the voting shares to the Gorsedd. They could be voted off the board, of course, by the electorate, but that's hardly likely as long as the shares are showing a decent profit. Interesting, really, as a social experiment. If times got really bad you'd find the electorate ganging up to get their own nominees on the board. Good God! Party politics, in fact. You'd not just be starting a completely revolutionary business venture: you'd be launching the first truly democratic state since Classical Greece.'

'And I'll have time for fishing?'

'Delegation, Sir Huw. Secret of all professional chairmanships.'

'But supposing things did get rocky?' ap Coch was a little alarmed to see that a suggestion that he had advanced so lightly was being taken so seriously. He reflected, not for the first time, that it was better not to make jokes to Sir Huw. He was too apt to turn them into courses of action.

'Well, d'you know,' his chieftain said. 'It mightn't be such a bad thing if we did have people like Jenkyn in. After all, there would be older heads to temper his wilder schemes. I mean, look at that chap he used to run around with in the early days. The schoolmaster, Meredith ap Owen. Never thought too much of him with his rantings. Then he got us to finance an Institute of Celtic Studies. Pointed out there wasn't one in the whole of Wales. Must confess, I didn't think much of the idea at the time. But it seemed a harmless enough way of cocking a snook at Cardiff.'

'Yes,' agreed ap Coch. 'And what a success he's made of that. International reputation, travelling scholarships. Celtic festivals at Lugnasad, bringing in winter visitors when everyone else is going broke building conference halls.'

'And talking of poacher turned game-keeper,' said Fort, 'what about that old rascal Meredith Raisin Balls? Never thought I'd see the day when he'd become warden of a Wildlife Sanctuary doing visiting lectureships to zoology students at UCNW. I suppose the lesson is that it's a question of channelling talent. Like a stream really. If you dam it up it overflows its banks and creates havoc. But let it run in its natural direction and it's no trouble to anyone.'

'Not even Effyngham-Blynd.'

They all roared. The marriage of Sir Pelham to Miss Magersfontein Blair had been one of the more bizarre results of Tad's independence. As frequently happens late in life to spinsters of both sexes the marriage had been an outstanding success. And since the couple bathed in the soothing waters of mutual esteem they were blithely ignorant of the hilarity of those who watched them from the bank. Lady Effyngham-Blynd, as she now was, had delighted her proud husband with an impressive pedigree which linked him both with an Elizabethan admiral and a medieval sept of one of the Royal Tribes of Wales, the bblynds. As a wedding gift and in reparation of his cruel jibe about life-renters, ap Gryfydd, in his role of King of Tad and the Islands, had created Sir Pelham a knight baronet of Tad, an hereditary title, and the College of Arms had been induced to admit his claim to the quartered arms of Effyngham and the barbarous device of the bblynds, three sightless Saxon heads, gules on a field or. He, in his turn, had used his considerable administrative gifts to turn their business of souvenir charters into a flourishing concern which gave the housewives of Byndrynkin pleasant and lucrative part-time employment colouring miniature achievements of arms. These sold readily among holiday-makers with Welsh names in their ancestry, linking them in spirit with the Happy Isles of Tad and Becod.

'That's something I forgot to mention,' ap Gryfydd recalled when the laughter died. 'There's another wedding loomin' up. My Ceri's back and that young dog Crisp. Got engaged last night.'

He paused, considering.

'Tell ye what, Fort. I don't think ap Coch's was such a bad idea. After all, it was his suggestion that Tad should seek UDI in the first place.'

Once more he paused considerately while ap Coch spluttered in mid-drink.

'If you're game to get out a prospectus and come on the board to advise us how to run things . . . well, dammit, I'm game to have a go at Tad & Co.'

'I'm game,' cried Fort with relish.

And so it happened.

ENVOI

Far away in gloomy London the Cabinet was meeting. It was not a pretty sight. A body of men and women, born each of them with a silver knife in their backs, had come together in their usual mood of back-slapping acrimony. The business on the agenda had been completed and the talk had drifted, as it always did, to the subject of Tad.

'But couldn't we buy some shares?' the Prime Minister asked plaintively. 'I believe their last dividend was phenomenal.'

The Chancellor of the Exchequer shook his head mournfully. ''Fraid not,' he said. 'Tried, of course, but they're fully subscribed and my understanding is that there is unlikely to be a further issue. Though there may be trouble in the future. Had I been asked I would have made transfer of the shares conditional on the recipient being a national of Tad. Theoretically there'd be nothing to stop outsiders buying in. Except, of course, it's difficult to envisage a situation where anyone would sell.'

'That good?'

'It's probably the most successful leisure enterprise in Western Europe,' the Minister for Trade explained. 'Hardly fail. All the employees are share-holders so they're not likely to go on strike. It would be cutting their own throats. Board of directors includes the island's leading Red and a millionaire capitalist, not to mention land-owners, businessmen and farmers. It's very expert indeed. And it has the advantage of the formidable administrator that the Prime Minister was pleased to give them.'

'Effyngham-Blynd, indeed!' the PM snorted savagely.

'Two bb' s now. Both lower case,' the Cabinet Secretary reminded the PM with scarcely less savagery. 'And a hereditary baronet.'

But the niceties of the Honours Game were of little

moment to any of the Cabinet. On the table before them lay the latest bureaucratic bomb-burst from the EEC's Central Policy Bureau. Since the Parliament had now extended its circuit, it met not only in Brussels, Strasbourg and Luxembourg. There were also sessions in Berlin, Paris and Amsterdam. But civil servants, tired with travel, had insisted that each parliamentary centre have its own Civil Service, duplicating that of the other centres.

'I suppose Tad's out of the Common Market long since, Foreign Secretary?'

'Not they, Prime Minister. Far too shrewd,' the lady addressed replied. 'You may remember that in the early 'seventies the UK negotiated a special membership deal for the Isle of Man. God alone knows why. We were on a good wicket, of course, since we got a share of the Common Purse. But it was the Isle of Man that did best. Frankly, the EEC were terrified that if they closed all the loopholes in places like the Isle of Man there would be a flight of capital to tax havens outside the Community. Anyway, the upshot was that the Isle of Man was granted membership of the Community and virtual exemption from the Treaty of Rome. Which means it can escape the tariff barriers yet still trade freely in Europe. But it is bound neither by constitutional nor fiscal ties. It has, in short, its Eurocake and not only eats it gleefully: it doesn't have to pay for it either.'

'Don't tell me,' the Prime Minister sighed. 'Tad used our negotiations for the Isle of Man as a precedent and got in on the same deal.'

'Precisely.'

'So they don't have to put up with nonsense like this.' The PM indicated the policy document with a gesture of distaste.

There were now two and a half million civil servants in the six centres of the EEC and the paperwork threatened to overwhelm the member states.

This latest had come from the Eurosong Bureau whose headquarters, mysteriously, were in Macao.

'FROM THE OFFICE OF THE DIRECTOR, EUROSONG (DISCRIMINATION DIVISION),' it started, and then went on:

'Performances of RULE BRITTANIA and ILKLA MOOR BA'AT 'AT are in direct contravention of the EEC's EUROSONG STANDARDISATION POLICY. A final policy document on national anthems has not yet been promulgated. But as an interim measure the songs above enumerated cannot be performed except under licence. These licences must be the subject of personal application at this office and will only usually be granted for performances of historical pageants under the guidelines set out in our leaflet PBX/248/796/43.'

The Prime Minister had never been so angry since the disclosure that the President of the Board of Trade was a colonel in the KGB.

'There'll be hell to play when the Sovereign hears about this. And the people aren't going to like it either. You know what fuss there was when the Marseillaise went into the TOP TEN, EUROWIDE.'

'Only because they cheated,' the Foreign Secretary intervened hotly. 'They floated a secret subsidy and bought up every copy on the market. Naturally they sold the most copies that week. They'd brought out a new version in eight million pressings.'

'Can't we get out of the damned Market? Or, better still, re-negotiate our entry using Tad as a precedent? Dammit, we got them in.'

At nineteen, the new Attorney General was the youngest lady ever to hold the office. For that reason she seldom spoke at Cabinet meetings. She coughed discreetly. The rest of the Cabinet looked at her crossly.

'I was just wondering. Couldn't we invade Tad again and lose? Then they'd have to occupy us and give us billions in lovely aid to rebuild our shattered industries. You know, like we did with Germany?'

The Prime Minister looked at her in wonder.

'Out of the mouths of babes and sucklings . . . I want a meeting convened with the Chiefs of Staffs committee for this afternoon.' A pause and a suspicious glare round the table. 'I suppose none of you are CIA? Good. We don't want the Americans muscling in on this.'

'There's just one thing,' said the Home Secretary, who remembered old jokes. 'I suppose there's no danger we might win?'

'Not a hope,' replied the Prime Minister with finality.